Outcasts of the Storm

Outcasts of the Storm

A Western Trio

DAN CUSHMAN

SAGEBRUSH
Large Print Westerns

Copyright © Golden West Literary Agency, 2004

First published in Great Britain by ISIS Publishing Ltd.,
First published in the United States by Five Star Westerns

Published in Large Print 2006 by ISIS Publishing Ltd.,
7 Centremead, Osney Mead, Oxford OX2 0ES,
United Kingdom,
by arrangement with
Golden West Literary Agency

The moral right of the author has been asserted

British Library Cataloguing in Publication Data
Cushman, Dan
    Outcasts of the storm: a western trio. –
    Large print ed. –
    (Sagebrush Western series)
    1. Western stories
    2. Large type books
    I. Title II. Cushman, Dan. Windigo Pass
    III. Cushman, Dan. Feminine touch
    813.5'4 [F]

ISBN 0–7531–7550–9 (hb)

Printed and bound in Great Britain by
T. J. International Ltd., Padstow, Cornwall

Table of Contents

Editor's Note

Dan Cushman first featured the character Comanche John, a Montana road agent, in "The Conestoga Pirate" in *Frontier Stories* (Winter, 44). In this adventure as well as in the next to appear, "No Gold on Boothill" in *Action Stories* (Summer, 45), he was called Dutch John. Now those two early stories can be found in *No Gold on Boothill* (Five Star Westerns, 2001). It wasn't until publication of "Comanche John — Dead or Alive!" in *Frontier Stories* (Winter, 46) that the character's name was changed to what it would remain in the numerous adventures that followed in various magazines and in three novels: *Montana, Here I Be* (Macmillan, 1950), *The Ripper from Rawhide* (Macmillan, 1952), and *The Fastest Gun* (Dell First Edition, 1955). All three of these Comanche John novels have been subsequently reprinted by Chivers Press, Ltd., in hard cover editions in the Gunsmoke series. In *The Adventures of Comanche John* (Five Star Westerns, 2002) and *The Return of Comanche John* (Five Star Westerns, 2003) all of the remaining stories about Comanche John with one exception were gathered together for the first time in book form. The exception is the last Comanche John story Dan Cushman wrote titled "Windigo Pass". It was the final Comanche John story Dan Cushman wrote and is included here in book form for the first time.

Windigo Pass

CHAPTER
ONE

Apprentice to the
Old Comanche

Winter was in the air. The black-whiskered man could smell it. He reined in his gunpowder roan pony and sat with his head tilted slightly back, his nose in the wind like an old woolly wolf's. The air was sharp from snow higher up in the hills; it smelled of autumn pines and chokecherries. It smelled of the long cold to come. It made him shake a chill from his shoulders and fasten the tie strings of his deer-hide jacket.

"Birds of the air have their nests," he muttered. "Even the lone coyote has his den in the rocks. But the pore son o' woman hath nowhar to lie his head. Parson, ye hit it nigh on the nail head."

The parson was nowhere around. He was away off somewhere, cleaning the wickedness out of Last Chance, or Blackfoot City, or one of those other Sodom and Gomorrah gold camps, but the black-whiskered man addressed him anyway, feeling the need to talk away his lonesomeness.

He chewed tobacco, and spat, and wiped his lips on the back of his hand, and repeated the words over again, liking their Biblical sound. "No, they have naught whar to lie their head. By damn, I'm done with this lone-wolfing it. I'm grown sick of no stew in the kettle, and not even a kettle. This year I'm going to find me a Blackfeet gal and settle down."

He was shorter and broader than most men, and he had a way of sitting down on his pony that made him seem shorter and broader still. He had barbered his hair and whiskers with a Bowie knife, and it was not what would be called a smooth job. It was, in fact, downright ragged.

He wore a black slouch hat. His jacket was Sioux buckskin; his shirt had been linsey, blue once, but now grayish. He wore natural-mix homespun pants thrust into the tops of jackboots. The boots were pulled above his knees to protect him from the thorns that grew in tangles, choking every gulch in Montana Territory. Around his waist on crossed belts, hitched high for riding, was a brace of Navy sixes, Colt manufacture, .36 caliber. He carried a Bowie, too, and a powder and ball dispenser, and in a scabbard beneath his saddle a Jager rifle.

He rode at a slow amble, his eyes watchful, and he sang in a sort of quavering monotone, the words bumped out of him by the movements of the horse:

> Oh, gather 'round, ye teamster men
> And listen unto me,
> Whilst I sing of old Comanche John,
> The fastest gun thar be.
> He robs the coach, he robs the bank,

He robs the Union mail,
And he's left his private graveyards
All along the Bannack Trail.

He rode down a gulch, a very deep one, with high mountain ridges on both sides. He stopped singing. The stage road was just ahead. It dropped down one ridge, crossed the creek, and climbed again. High above he could see the road, switchbacking, exposing the sand rock of the mountain, gray-white like the cheap salt that was lately being freighted up from the Salt Lake for use in processing the silver ores of Ruby City.

At the creek he drew up. He stopped chewing, suspicion showing in the sag of his shoulders, and of his guns. There had been no sound, no movement, not even a smell of anything, but a streak of muddy water in the creek told him that someone, something, had crossed within the last five or ten minutes.

He sat and listened. The streak of mud slowly diluted and was carried away. He heard nothing. At last, he nudged the side of his pony, but not to follow the road, or even the trail he had been using. He chose a deep path through the brush.

He was 100 yards along this when the pony made a sudden twitch with his head up.

"Yep," he said quietly, "thar's *somebody*."

He dismounted. He limped some of the pain and stiffness from his legs. He seemed to be careless, slouched and sleepy, but he did not let a twig snap under his boots, and his eyes did not miss anything. Leaving his pony behind, he walked for a distance. He stopped. He had caught sight of a horse, a saddled and bridled horse, a large bay tied near the road.

He decided to wait for a while. He squatted down. He was there for about a minute when a man appeared. It was a tall young man with good shoulders. A blanket mostly covered him. He wore no hat, but a black kerchief was tied around his head so he could pull it down to make a mask. He was blond, the ruddy kind, not pale or washed out. He carried a brace of Navy pistols.

The young man kept moving around as though the soles of his boots were too hot for his feet. He kept looking this way and that and feeling of his pistols. One of the places he looked was up the mountainside, and there, among some rocks, was his hat, just its crown visible, and under it the twin muzzles of a sawed-off shotgun, the set-up made to look like he had a companion with a gun aimed. When the black-whiskered man changed position a little, he could see the road with a log across it for a barricade.

The black-whiskered man was critical, and a little sad. Obviously this fellow was poor shakes as a road agent. And the days of the poor-shakes road agent were short and full of bullet lead. No coach guard would be taken in by that hat-and-gun set-up on the hill, and it was too bad. It was, because this lad had a good, clean-cut look about him, he had a proud way with his shoulders, and he had the manner of a man who liked his horse.

Then, from far up the side of the gulch, came a clatter of hoofs and wheels. The coach was descending.

6

The young man looked frightened. He pulled his mask down, drew both Navies, and got out of sight.

He waited. It was quiet now, so quiet the sounds of the creek came through — the gurgle and echo of water over stones. The coach was passing through deep timber and it could be heard only when the road swung out around the rock faces of the mountain.

Suddenly it was there, with a loud creak and rattle. It was in view, top-heavy, careening to the creek, fording it out of sight briefly, then climbing again, water streaming from its wheels, the driver in the high seat, the shotgun guard beside him with a rifle clamped between his knees, a full load of passengers inside.

A bend in the road hid the obstruction until the last second. The lead team saw it and made a lunge off the road, into the chokecherry bramble. With a curse the driver was on his feet, going for the brake, hauling back with hands and forearms operating the lines.

"Hands up!" shouted the young man, getting himself into the road, his Navies angled upward at the driver and guard.

The coach stopped so suddenly it unbalanced the guard, almost threw him off the seat, and probably saved the robber's life. The teams were mixed with harness, climbing one another's rumps, and the driver with a mighty, cursing dexterity was getting them strung out.

To make things worse, some of the passengers were trying to get outside, some were trying to hide, and all of them were shouting at once.

7

"Hold it, or I'll fire!" cried the young man beneath mask and blanket, aiming at the driver.

"Damn ye, I'm doing my best!" He sat down with his boots braced and the brake on, having gee-hawed the teams into a zigzag sort of stability. "And don't p'int them guns at me, ye fool! Kill me and then who'll control these Injun mules?"

The young fellow called to the guard. "You get down!" The guard started to obey and slide his long, limber frame over the far side of the coach. "No, this side. Don't try anything." He waved back at the hillside, at the hat and gun muzzles. "I'm not alone."

The guard, hands uplifted, slid belly first to the ground. He had a chinless, sag-mouth face and from his place in the trees the black-whiskered man recognized him. Eads. Bill Eads. The black-whiskered man not only recognized him, he hated his yellow guts.

"Hold the horses!" said the young robber.

Eads still carried a gun. He had an Army model Colt tied down on his right leg. The weight of it made him seem to limp a trifle as he went forward, but he kept turned to hide the gun, and he succeeded.

The whiskered man, chewing nervously, whispered: "Git the gun, ye young idjit, git the gun!"

But he did not see the gun. He moved far over against the slant of the mountain where he tried to watch everybody at once.

"Climb out, all of you!" he called to the passengers.

A heavy, flushed man was the first to emerge. A couple of others followed; a seedy, dressed-up man; a spare, gray, brittle-looking, elderly man whose knees

8

seemed to pain him; a girl, very pretty, about nineteen years old; and there were two other men and a woman.

The girl's skirt had caught on the iron step. She tore it. The young road agent started forward, apparently with a gentleman's instinct that asserted itself even here.

"Stay away from me!" she cried.

The elderly gentleman freed her dress, took her arm, said some words of reassurance. They were very similar in profile and it was easy to guess that she was his daughter or granddaughter.

"Line up!" the robber said, swinging his Navies.

"Don't point your guns at me!" the girl cried. "Don't —"

"Nettie!" the gentleman said.

Eads, tall, double-jointed, and sag-jawed, was holding the lead team. His left side was in view. Very slowly he lowered his right hand, doing it with a snaky, smooth movement, straight down. It was hidden from the young man's view. Now, using only hand, wrist, and forearm, he lifted the revolver from its holster. He held it with the barrel toward the ground. He had yet to turn and point it. He started this very casually, looking not at his quarry, but at the horses. A half second more and the young road agent would have been a dead man.

The black-whiskered man drew and fired, a practiced movement, a hitch of his right shoulder, the blued shine of a Navy in his hand, an explosion and a whip of lead from the jack timber.

The guard was hit and knocked from his feet. He lay bullet-shocked with the team threatening to trample him.

"Stay whar ye be!"

The voice of the black-whiskered man stopped everyone. The young robber spun around.

"Stay on your job! Git back to it, lad. Now maybe they'll believe ye when ye tell 'em you're not alone."

Eads was on his right side, his bleeding right arm on the ground. He got hold of it and pressed down to stop the blood. He got groggily to his knees. He looked around, baffled.

"Hello, Bill," said the whiskered one.

Eads shook himself like one trying to awaken. He kept looking for the voice.

"Me, Bill. I'm hyar. Heered ye was riding shotgun. By grab, if I'd *knowed*, I'd have taken this coach myself, solo. I would have for a certainty."

"Who are you?" Eads cried.

"Forgot the voice? Ree-collect the old days in Californy, Sidewinder Gulch when the yaller gold was clogging the sluice and times was good with enough for all, and you and your stranglers laid in wait with your coward guns for poor Billy-Boy Garrity just for a thousand measly dollars of ree-ward money? Now ye remember? And do ye remember the one that got away?"

"Comanche John!"

"Why, yep, it be!" The black-whiskered man lowered his voice in reverence to his old-time reputation. "Yep, it's the old Comanche in person. Do ye hear that, one of ye and all? This be Comanche John, the man they wrote the song about. So step lively and watch your manners and do what the lad tells ye, because I've just tooken him on as apprentice to teach him my art and my craft, because it's a fact that one of these days the gold trails will see me no more. Glory be, I've hit the sawdust trail. I've tooken religion, and I'm headed northward for the land of the Blackfeet whar I aim to ree-tire and settle down."

CHAPTER
TWO

Sour on the World

Comanche John hunkered and chewed. He had a Navy ready, but he didn't expect he'd have to use it. He picked at his teeth with a spear of grass and looked at the lad with a critical eye.

The young fellow was nervous with no idea how to conduct a robbery, no idea at all. When necessary, John dropped a word of advice, but quietly, not wanting to embarrass him.

"Keep the coach door open. Make 'em line up straight. Military."

The driver, craning, was trying to get a glimpse of John: "Say, you robbed me down in I-dee-ho."

"Could be." He went on instructing: "Lad, forgit about the small truck. They ain't my style. Fetch the strongbox. Not you, let one of the men do it. I do hope it ain't riveted to the floor because that'd mean burning the coach."

The box was not riveted down. One of the miners dumped it to the ground. There was no use demanding the key because it would be at the express office in Jackson City.

"Tell 'em to git in and git," John said, and in another minute the coach, with all back aboard, was rolling away, pulling the steep mountain grade.

Comanche John thereupon slouched into view.

"Son," he said, "you might have got kilt."

The young man did not answer. He pulled off his kerchief, revealing a face beaded and streaked with sweat. He was too trembly to stand. He sat down on a rock and breathed, steadying himself.

John said: "Put the Navies back before they explode and blow your toes off."

He did, poking several times to find the holsters. Finally he was able to speak. "You really Comanche John?"

"Yep, I be. But don't mind that. Don't let it excite ye. Famous men are about the same as any other once ye git to know 'em."

The young fellow laughed with a bitter jerk of his shoulders. "Now I suppose you'll rob *me*. It serves me right."

"Me take all the swag? Why, how you talk. Share and share alike is my motto. Leastwise this coach. No gold. Greenbacks, maybe, if we're lucky. Incoming coach, ye see."

They pried the strongbox open. It contained neither money nor bullion — nothing of value but a few trinkets addressed to a jeweler in Ruby City, over the Windigo Pass.

Comanche John sat down on the box in disgust and said: "Son, what possessed ye to choose this coach?"

"I took my chance. The first . . ."

"I should have let him shoot ye. I should have."

They rode away together, the young man tall and straight in the saddle, the older one giving and sagging with each move of his horse. They followed the brush of the bottoms, and then a deer trail up the mountain.

The coach was long since out of sight. The sun shone pale for a while, then it faded among clouds near the horizon. As they climbed, a cold wind found them. It was a frigid reminder of the lateness of the season, making Comanche John hide his hands inside his jacket to keep them warm.

When they stopped to breathe their horses, he said: "I can see I got a heap o' work on my hands teaching you to be a coach robber. You don't look like the type. Not that that's anything ag'in' you."

"It wasn't robbery in one way of looking at it."

"Eh?"

"The coach was partly mine by rights. My name is Pelton. They call me Buck. Buck Pelton."

"Pelton of Hames and Pelton?"

The young man nodded.

"You ain't old Rawhide Pelton's boy?"

"Yes." He brightened. "Say, are you a friend of Dad's?"

"That's not quite the word for it." Comanche John looked at him balefully and took his hands from his jacket to feel along the smooth-worn Navy butts. "Fact is, you being his boy don't recommend you to me a-tall. That damn' Rawhide Pelton was the first man to put sleeper guards inside his stagecoaches disguised as honest passengers."

14

"All's fair in . . ."

"And I say *no*. All ain't fair. There's a right and a wrong way to everything, a brave way and a sneakin' way, and I say a sleeper guard is a low, ornery trick on a road agent. O' course, I speak unbiased, seeing I give up coach robbery, took religion, hit the sawdust trail, figuring on finding me a Blackfeet gal and spending my last years in peace. Got nothing at stake. Just like to see things run on the square. And when I think of poor old Tom Tate, lying dead in his grave on Sky-U road, riddled with buckshot by a sleeper guard on your pappy's coach! Made up a verse about him. Teamsters did. Verse in my song. You heered my song, haven't ye?"

Young Pelton shook his head.

"Ignorance. Young man, I can see ye won't git along too well in this country, got no mind to principle, no thought to the important people, trail blazers, men that chased out the Injuns. Now, pay heed and I'll sing a bit to ye."

They rode on, following a trail through sparse timber, around a big bulge of the mountain, with the black-whiskered man singing.

> Thar was Comanche John and Silcox
> And Buckshot Tommy Tate,
> And before the autumn it was o'er
> They all had met their fate;
> They shot Silcox in Denver,
> And poor Tommy got the same,
> Whilst Comanche took religion
> And tried to change his name.

15

John stopped, blasted tobacco juice into the wind, and explained: "Smith's the name I been going under. Then, betimes, I use another name, Jones. They're both good, but I think I prefer Smith to Jones. It's not so unusual. That's another thing ye got to pay heed to when ye take up robbery as a profession."

The trail was wider here, and they rode stirrup to stirrup.

John went on talking, his head down, the wind bending his black slouch hat over his face. "A man does have to be careful about the names he picks. Say ye choose to call yourself by an unusual name like Beauregard. Well, right off, if there happens to be another Beauregard within three sleeps and two mountain ranges, he can't rest until he's off to see ye and find out if you're of the New Orleans Beauregards or the Natchez Beauregards, and right off he learns that you're neither. But the Smiths don't care, and it's been my motto that the Joneses don't give a damn, neither."

They rode into a wind that precluded conversation, that caught words and whipped them away so a man had to shout to be heard. The wind carried pellets of snow that stung when they hit. Finally the trail turned and reached the ridge top, and they rode westward with their backs to protect them.

"I'm not a snooper," Comanche John said, "but I must say I'm a bit curious what a Pelton was doing out robbing one of his own stagecoaches."

"They were half and half, my dad and Lawford Hames. Dad was sick, came to Saint Louis to be doctored. I was in the Army. When they discharged me

16

with a rifle ball in my hip, I heard that the company was bankrupt. I suspected Hames then, but Dad didn't. He blamed himself, his sickness, said it was because he wasn't on the job to help. He said that Hames was honest, he'd stake his life on it. I almost believed him. I went to Denver City when I was able to, thought I could save something. We'd been sold out. In the meantime Hames went to Idaho and started a freight and stage line of his own. Coaches, express, gold buyer . . . a real big man."

"And you're here after him?"

Pelton nodded. He looked big in the jaw, narrow-eyed, determined.

"So ye picked on a Hames coach. Any particular thing you were looking for?"

"No. I wanted to get back at him somehow."

"And if I hadn't come along, ye'd have been dead. It's a fact, Pelton, with your style I'd hate to trust ye with the robbery of anything except a Chinee washee."

Pelton laughed. He had a very pleasant laugh. Every time he laughed, it made the whiskered man feel good. John said: "That varmint Lawford Hames! It just makes me bile. Here was his partner, sick in Saint Loo, and his partner's own son in the Army, out fighting for the Confed'racy . . ."

"The Union."

Comanche John turned away from him. He had grown sour on the world. He slapped his old, black hat flatter on his head and blasted tobacco juice at a porphyry boulder and cursed. "Why is it," he said, "when I come riding along, and see some ignorant

17

nobody trying to rob a coach, ready to be kilt . . . when I see something like that, why don't I just go along and mind my own business? Now here's a fellow . . ." — he flung an arm out at Pelton, addressing not his horse, but just the mountain in general — "he's a damn' Yank, son of the man that dead-falled my best friend, a fellow so damn' ignorant he's not even heered the most popular song in the whole Nor'west, and I save him, rescue him, when by all the laws of judgment and good decency I ought to kill him myself. By grab, I *do* need a squaw to take care o' me, because it looks like my brains have jellied."

Pelton allowed his horse to lag a short distance so he could laugh about it. He choked off the laugh, however, and placed a glum expression on his face when Comanche John cast a glance back at him.

"Don't sulk, damn ye," said John. "If they's one thing I can't abide, it's a sulking man. Anyhow it ain't your fault you're a damn' Yank. It's the way you was brung up."

They rode side-by-side as it became dark. The snow was light, only an edging of white on the icy sides of boulders, and some early stars were visible through it.

Comanche John reined in, hooked his leg around the saddle horn, and indicated a direction with a spurt of tobacco juice.

"Thar's Jackass City. See, that bunch o' lights yonder."

The lights were many miles away, beyond some foothills, across a valley, against the blackness of a

18

timbered mountainside. Still higher in the background was a craggy ridge, purplish and snow-capped.

He pointed to a notch in the ridge. "Windigo Pass. Ruby on t'other side. Not far, eight, ten mile. Ruby. Plenty will be heard o' Ruby. She'll be the biggest silver camp north of the Comstock when the veins deep down are opened. Ruby silver, I've seen it, big as so, red as blood and heavy as bullet metal. That's what Hames is aiming for . . . Ruby, and not that poor-scratch camp o' Jackass City. I 'low there'll be three thousand men in Ruby come next spring. And that gives me an idee. No, no . . . just forget I said anything."

He kept thinking about the silver mines of Ruby, however, and about young Pelton whose family had long been interested in the freight business.

"Great opportunity, lad," he said.

Buck Pelton rode close to him, listening for him to go on.

"They'll need heavy-freight quicksilver, salt, amalgamators, stamp mills, cable, stuff like that. Great opportunity for a freighting man."

"They have a freighting man," Buck said with bitterness, thinking of Lawford Hames.

"But he don't know the country, not like me." John pointed to the high snow ridge beyond Jackass as he talked. "Now, I been yonder and back again, and I learned a thing or three. I learned about Windigo Pass."

"If it's a good road, then Hames is using it."

"That's just the point. It's no road at all."

Hames, said John, was using the Elk Creek road. Now the Elk Creek was fine, except that it took the

19

long, winding way around, and was always snowed-in deep in winter — but the Windigo!

"You mean I could grab the Windigo route for myself?" Buck Pelton asked.

"Why, that depends on you, but I could show ye the way, straight and true across the hump, old Injun trail, steep but blown clear except for half a mile whar ye'd need snow sheds."

Pelton suddenly reined in. "What mining company is it in Ruby . . . the London & Montana?"

"Why, yes, I do believe . . ."

"Of course! The London & Montana! That's why he came here."

"Hames?"

"The agreement . . . the one Dad signed."

"Lad, you're talking all around me."

"The Pelton and Hames company had an agreement with them. They were headed into new territory and needed a freight agreement. Pelton and Hames guaranteed the wagons and they guaranteed the tonnage. My dad put the deal through. Now Hames is here to put the old contract in force."

John cried: "Lad, I just thought of something, if you . . ."

"Of course, it's as much my contract as Hames's. And you're in it with me, half and half."

"Me? In what?"

"In the freight business."

John chewed it over as he rode. "Me in the freight business," he muttered. "Why, sure. I had experience on the road. Office, spring-seated chair. Desk and a

20

spittoon. Black serge suit and congress gaiters. Why, sure, I can just see me now. We'll beat that cheating Lawford Hames at his own game."

"We'll break him, and then I'll break his neck."

"We'll whipsaw him and flim-flam him and we'll weight him with lead from a Navy Colt. Go tell the Blackfeet maidens to wait because I got one last fling in my hide and I'm going to cut myself a slice of fortune whilst making it." Comanche John flanked the gunpowder pony that bucked and almost threw him. "Yipee!" he shouted to the cold mountain air. "I'm a ring-tailed ripper from the Rawhide Mountains! I been riding down the narrow path of rectitude so long my gun barrel is rusty, so git out o' my way, ye freight tycoons, because I got it in my mind to pall-bear a couple of funerals!"

CHAPTER
THREE

Jackass City

They came to the road and followed it. As they descended, the snow disappeared and became a trickle of water in the ruts. In the valley bottom it was mud. They followed a creek whose water was thick yellow from placer workings higher up. Prospectors' shanties and dugouts had been built along the sides of the gulch. The road climbed through pines, dropped over a shoulder of ground, and there were the lights of Jackass City.

It was a larger camp than John had expected, for it had boasted only a dozen cabins on the last visit. Placer mining had spread from the gulch bottom to the benches and had pushed the town up the slope, here and there undermining the main street itself so trestles or log crib works were necessary to keep it from caving in. The chief building of the town was a two-story stone and log structure topped by a sign so large it could be read during the dark of night — **THE OVERLAND HOTEL.**

"That's us," said Pelton.

"It ain't me," said John. "I don't like to git hemmed in."

"Freight moguls, we got to act the part."

They rode warily down the main street. It was cold with only a few people about, hurrying from one place to another. Apparently there was no excitement because of the robbery. The hoof-punched muck of the street had commenced to freeze, but not deeply, only at the surface, enough to make a brittle sound under the hoofs of the horses.

On the main corner, between a pine mast and the top of the Overland Hotel, a street lamp burned. It was too high to be effective, and had been erected for style, but John was more wary than ever riding beneath it, and he kept warming one hand and then the other inside his jacket, keeping them ready for the gun butts, but no one paid the slightest attention to them. A hundred yards farther on they found a feed corral and tapped the wagon-tire gong for service.

A young Negro, smartly attired in a steamboat officer's uniform, came from the shack and let the gate down. Under questioning, he told them that the stagecoach had been robbed again.

"Ag'in?" cried John. "What's the country coming to? Who's the sheriff here? Ain't we got a vigilance committee, a miners' meeting? Why'n't the law clean these varmints out? I dunno whether I feel safe in this town or not. You keep my horse saddled, understand? Take the saddle off, and curry him, and feed him, and put it back on again. I got an idee I'll just be passing through."

He limped from the stiffness of long riding in the cold, and was still limping when they went downhill to the plank sidewalk in front of the Overland. A high, ornate awning had been attached to the front of the building, and there were green-painted benches for guests to sit on, but nobody was there tonight. The front windows were misted over. John lagged behind his companion, letting him reach the door first, and go inside first.

"I got no fancy for this place," John said.

The lobby was low and wide with a huge pillar in the middle. Most of the light came from bracket lamps on the four sides of the pillar. Nine or ten men were seated in the big chairs on the lounge side of the room, dripping mud off their boots and spitting tobacco juice wherever they pleased, doing it in a prosperous way which showed them to be mine owners, boss freighters, or at the very least paying guests.

John did not recognize a soul.

"Four walls, thick ones, too. Last time I saw walls this thick it war a jail, and I war in it."

A small, quick-eyed man dressed all in black except for his shirt had appeared behind the desk.

"I assume, sir," said Buck Pelton, looking him coldly in the eye, "that dinner is still available."

The man straightened, recognizing quality when it appeared before him, and said: "Oh, yes, on special order, sir! Would you like to register for rooms, sir?"

Comanche John looked all around, his black slouch hat far over his eyes, not chewing very hard, his face pulled in on itself as though to hide it still more deeply behind the black whiskers.

"What's your charges?" he asked.

24

"Ten dollars a night." Then the clerk added: "Unless you want the cheaper rooms, then . . ."

"Cheaper! Hell's fire, who ye think you're talking to?" He shot tobacco juice at a brass spittoon, and missed it. "Poor grade o' spittoon . . . I dunno. That price, it's pretty low to what we been used to. Me and my partner, we're big freight operators, backed by British capital, naturally used to the best. I'd guess we should sample the grub hereabouts first."

The clerk said, "As you wish," and pointed the way to the dining room.

"You carried that off in fine style," said young Pelton.

"Oh, I been around a mile or three in my time. Been in San Francisco, Denver City, Hannibal. Not much of a man for hotels. Feather beds. Too soft. Bend a man in the middle, weaken his spine. Don't do a gun barrel a bit o' good to bend in the middle, and neither does it a man's spine. You know what the best bed in the world is? Spruce boughs with a buffalo robe on good mountain soil. You lie on a bed like that, real straight, with your toes pointed down, and ye can feel the tiredness pick up and flow out of ye whilst your body sucks new strength out of the soil. I've done it many a night."

John talked to fill the time while walking to the dining room. He discarded his chaw and looked around. The men were still watching, but not in a crafty way, just relaxed and gossipy, so things were all right. From some distant portion of the building they could hear a violin, flute, and harp playing polka music, so he surmised that there was a dance hall and saloon portion

25

of the building, but separated off with private entrances as befitted a first-class traveler's hotel.

They passed through a cloak closet. Buck hung up his sheared beaver hat, but John kept his black slouch on — it was part of his disguise.

The main dining room had a single, large table down the middle. Places were all set, the plates upside down, with napkins, knives, and forks ready for breakfast. There was an arch and a second dining room beyond — the quality dining room with private tables, and up some steps to a slightly higher level a row of booths with silk screens that could be folded out for privacy.

A Chinese boy came running up to say: "Private table, sure, much obliged, come quick, please."

"We getting mighty deep in this cave," John muttered, but they followed him.

One of the booths was occupied. Comanche John, shorter and lagging behind, felt Buck's hesitation of surprise and guessed who it would be. It was the girl and the old gentleman of the stagecoach, and there was a third person, a very strong-shouldered man of medium age who had been talking in a spirited manner.

The man stopped. He seemed startled, just as Buck Pelton was startled.

John said from the side of his mouth: "Ye danged fool, don't let on ye recognize 'em. Get ye a road-agent sign if ye like. Have one printed, hang it around your neck."

"It's all right." He walked on a few steps and said: "Hello, Hames."

John took a good breath. Of course, this was Hames, the former partner. This was Hames's hotel, too. That was the reason for it, a grand place in a medium camp, to accommodate passengers bound across the range to Ruby.

"Well, Buck!" Hames sounded delighted. He looked it, too. He smiled, showing his strong teeth only slightly stained by tobacco. He had a mustache, clipped short, and no beard; the mustache added force to the smile, like a red-brown line drawn over it.

John hung back, not watching Hames so much as the girl and the old gentleman.

The old man was smiling politely. No recognition there. But the girl — she was too smart and too pretty. For a homely woman was one thing and a pretty woman was something else, and John had never known anything but trouble from a pretty woman.

Hames was introducing Buck to the girl and the old gentleman. He was explaining to them that Buck, dear Buck, was the son of his former partner. She was Miss Nettie Bowden, of San Francisco. All the while he talked, Hames kept moving his heavy, graceful body around behind the chairs, watching for trouble, while pretending that trouble was the furthest thing from his mind.

Comanche John took note of the exits, the one leading somewhere upstairs, the one that must lead to a kitchen, and, of course, the one they had just come through.

Someone had followed them. He turned, saw the man, and experienced a bad jolt. The man was Moose

Petley. Yes, big, powerful Moose Petley, the same Moose Petley who should have been dead back at Big Hole Pass.

Buck was introducing him and John awakened to the fact just as he said: "My partner, Mister Jones."

"Smith," said John. "And I just now happen to ree-collect I got important business back at the corral. Durned if I didn't come hyar to supper without my white linen shirt on."

Buck told him to wait. John moved back, watching Moose Petley, and watching the folks in the booth. Moose suddenly disappeared. It might have been his spirit, maybe risen from the dead. That might be. If so, John didn't particularly mind, because Moose Petley was one man he'd rather have dead than alive.

Hames moved toward Buck, a troubled look on his face. "Buck!" he said. "There's no hard feelings! Now shake hands with me."

Buck looked coldly at his outstretched hand and said: "I wouldn't be a big enough hypocrite for that."

He said it courteously, and that made it seem worse. Hames stopped as though he'd been slapped. He carried a small, pearl-handled, European pistol at the opening of his coat, and a whip with a loaded butt was ready in his right coat pocket. He moved his hands in a brushing motion as if reaching for both, but his hand remained empty. He looked Buck in the eyes. Through tight lips he said: "You pup! You say that after all I did for you, kept the outfit on wheels, you in that Saint Louis college and me paying the bills, supporting your father all those years while he turned himself into a hopeless drunk . . ."

Buck started for him. Hames, seizing the whip, fell back a step. Comanche John tripped Pelton, and, when Hames started to swing, his target was no longer there. Instead, he saw the black-whiskered man with a Navy unholstered — not pointed, but ready.

"Put it away," said Comanche John. "Put the whip away, Hames, or I'll slice it off right next to your hand, I will for a fact, and whips of that Spanish quality ain't come by at every cross-trail trading post."

Hames was taut and furious. He did not like to take an order. Not even from a man with a gun in his hand, not even to save his life. He hesitated; for a second he seemed about ready to come on with the whip anyway, then he exhaled, and forced a smile across his lips, and coiled the whip, and put it away again.

He turned then, bowed stiffly to the girl and her father, and said: "I'm very sorry."

The old gentleman, Mr. P. R. Bowden, was on his feet, angry, his face grayer than ever except for two spots of color on his cheeks. "Sir, if it's because of my daughter and myself that you are tolerating this, we will . . ."

"His father meant a great deal to me," Hames said.

The old gentleman sat down again at the table. Hames apologized again briefly, and called the Chinese boy who closed the screen in front of the booth.

CHAPTER
FOUR

Soft in his Old Age

"We better git," said John. He didn't like the look on Hames's face. Hames wasn't the type you crossed and walked away from with your back turned. The day that the meek inherited the earth Hames would be left a pauper.

Buck Pelton had turned his ankle when John tripped and hipped him to the floor; now he was standing, holding the back of a chair, saying: "What the devil did you knock me down for? I was about to . . ."

"You was about to get carved down the middle and crosswise with that whip."

John urged him back toward the archway to the main dining room. He kept watching for Moose Petley. It occurred to him that Moose Petley was probably on Hames's payroll. He went through the arch half expecting an ambush blast from one of the shadowy corners.

Buck still cursed him, and John said: "Hush and be quiet."

"What's the trouble?"

"I seen a ghost."

That closet yonder, it would be Petley's style to wait there in ambush. Unless he *was* a ghost, and John did not much believe in ghosts. Back in Pike County they had ghosts, it had been proved a hundred times, but there they had old, established graveyards, and decayed houses to haunt, things a ghost really needed if he was going to be anything, while hereabouts a man never heard of ghosts. It *was* Moose, no spirit about him, it was Moose in the body. After all, John had never *seen* him dead and under the dirt. He had only taken folks' word for it. Wagon talk, teamster talk. Loud-mouth teamster talk. He cursed all teamsters for liars.

He was ready for Moose Petley as he passed through the cloak closet, and again when he entered the lobby, but Petley was not waiting. Men were there, the same men as before, yawning, talking, digging wax from their ears with matchsticks — those Blue Devil patent matches that lately were becoming commonplace in the gold camps.

"Why is it," John drawled as if Petley were the furthest thing from his mind, "when a man gits prosperous, the first thing he does is loaf in a hotel lobby and dig the wax from his ears?" He held Buck closely as they went outside and said: "Easy, now."

"What's the trouble?"

"Petley. I seen him yonder. Time was when he was a whiskey trader amongst the Paiutes. Renegade. Big fellow with an ox-yoke mustache."

"Does he know you?"

"You're tootin' right he knows me."

"He could get you hanged then."

31

"Hung, ye mean? Plenty o' men thought they could git *me* hung." He said it deeply in his throat, from one side of his mouth, and he watched for any suspicious movement along the street.

A rangy wolf-dog had come sniffing along at the corners and now he stopped with ears cocked to look in the shadow between two small, long-shanty saloons.

"I'll bet ye!" said John.

He ambled that way, down from the Overland's platform wall, along a stretch of pole corduroy, almost to where the dog was standing.

John, close against the building, spoke: "Moose, come out o' thar or I'll drill ye right betwixt the eyes."

He could hear a startled movement. Then slowly the huge fellow plodded out of the darkness, along the narrow space hardly wide enough for his shoulders.

"Why, it's my old friend, John," said Moose. "I didn't know who you were."

"The hell you didn't."

"On my soul, no, I didn't."

"Why were ye waiting to bushwhack me?"

"I wasn't. I had plenty of chance to bushwhack you at the hotel if I'd been that kind. Oh, I kilt a couple of men in my time, might as well own up to it, but honest, fair, and square, bullets in front, toe-to-toe. I mayn't ever had religion, but I got my code."

John spat. He kept watch of him. He looked Moose up and down, all six feet two, 200 pounds of him. He still had a hunch Moose was working for Hames.

"What were you doing inside that hotel?"

"I live there!"

"Oh, live there be damned! Look at ye . . . haven't had a bath since ye fell overboard in the Sacremento back in 'Fifty-four. Lice on ye . . ."

"It's a lie. I bathed just last year at that barber shop down in Boise City."

"I know first-class livery barns that wouldn't tolerate a man like you sleeping in their stalls, let alone a hotel like the Overland. I know why you was thar . . . ye be working for Hames."

Moose Petley opened his mouth to say — "No." — but he didn't say it. He simply left it gaping with surprise at John's having guessed the truth.

"I should shoot ye," John muttered, angry at his own softness. "I should and put it down as my good deed for the day."

"You wouldn't do that, John. We been through too much together. Sometimes we been on opposite sides, true, but we been through it. Old friends is the best friends. I always say, I learned my lesson at Big Hole. I'm a changed man. I'll admit my mistake. I'll admit I fell in with bad companions . . . Dave Royal, Belly River George, and that lot . . . but I learned my lesson. I'm still carrying rifle lead from the Big Hole to remind me of that lesson. I tell ye, Comanche . . ."

"Name ain't Comanche. Name is Smith, or Jones. I don't care much which. You go shouting Comanche around hyar and git me hung, why I'll see to it you're hung, too. I could do it."

"I know you could do it," Moose said, pleading, "but men with marks ag'in' their names have to stick together. I'll keep quiet about it if you'll keep quiet."

Moose wanted to buy them a drink but the offer was refused.

"I don't trust him," said Buck.

"I *trust* him," John muttered, meaning he'd trust him to shoot him in the back.

They rode from camp, found an abandoned dugout shanty, and slept for a while. They got up and cooked breakfast. The camp was misty and gray below them with the smokes of early fires hanging in the treetops, spreading down the gulch. In the other direction they could see the cold mountains of the Windigo.

"Our pass!" said Buck, and there was doubt in his voice. It looked steep and forbidding.

"Yep, our pass!"

They rode up the gulch, along a wagon road, to a cluster of cabins called Stumptown where some poor quartz veins were being developed. The road played out in half a dozen directions on the other side of Stumptown, and the two men found themselves in a grassy, *cirque*-like area with the mountain rising steeply on three sides.

"Main camp could be here," John said.

They rode on, along a trail. This, John pointed out, could be widened to make a road. He talked about Ruby, over the pass, about the huge silver mines that British capital was developing, and about silver mines in general.

"I war at Comstock. Learned all about silver mines. Mills, pan amalgamators, stamps, hot steam jets, all that truck. Tell ye why they have to have our road, the year-around road . . . because something breaks down once a day and a steady stream of repair parts has to come or the mine goes bust. Knew a hold-up man one time, used to waylay repair parts, hold 'em for ransom. Only one day he got a box marked rush . . . enjine bearings . . . and it war fifty pounds of giant powder on a time fuse."

Steep as it was, John pointed out at their first rest that the Windigo was *the* winter road because much of it would blow clear, and the bad places, where snow would settle in forty or fifty feet deep, were short and could be tunneled by snowsheds. Of course, there were the cliffs. Over the cliffs they'd need to trestle.

"Build all that *this fall?*"

"I got friends. I got friends with more muscle and less brains than anybody you'd likely come onto this side of Ioway."

John had his mind on some flat-broke wagon emigrants whose hide he had saved on the Big Hole. They were settled at White Pine Valley and had shotgunned some crops, but, unless things had changed, they hadn't harvested much except children. Even the dumbest of them, a man like Ambrose Stocker, could dig a road and build a trestle and keep snow shoveled and make himself a few dollars charging toll if somebody with brains told him how.

"The Pelton-Comanche Wagon Lines," said John. "Now, that *sounds* like something."

"I thought the *Comanche* was secret."

"Not after I git up in the world. I notice they never wave rope at a man of property."

They rode on. The mountain became steeper. They switchbacked toward a high peak from which the early snow had not melted. Great blocks of porphyry here covered the slope.

"There's a job for your farmers," said Buck.

"Nothing to it. Show 'em how. Snake-hole the big ones, jump-shoot the smaller ones, giant powder, roll 'em down the hill."

"Where do we get giant powder?"

"On credit from Ruby."

Here it was alternating timber and stone. Glaciers of another age had scooped out a three-sided amphitheater with cliffs for walls. Far below lay a tiny lake.

"No place for a road here," Buck said.

"Why, no. You ree-collect I said something about a trestle? Two hundred paces of trestle here saves ye six miles. And that, son, is one of the ways we'll beat Hames. Oh, I can just see that Hames wallowing tail-deep on his mules up that Elk Creek road and hyar we'll be, the Pelton-Comanche Freight Lines rolling safe and solid across trestle and through snowshed tunnel, putting out two hundred tons a day into Ruby regular like clockwork."

They crossed the pass and rode down to the new camp of Ruby. It didn't have a placer-camp look about it; it had a hard-rock look. In other words, you could tell there was capital at work. The London & Montana had set up a sawmill, so everything was built of plank rather than log. The streets had been laid off and things were going up in squares instead of just mushrooming everywhere. The whiskey, however, was as bad as anywhere.

John told them plenty about their whiskey while waiting for Buck to come back from his meeting with P. W. Hutton, resident manager of the London & Montana.

John waited a long time, and he expected the worst. "He tried to welsh on ye?" he asked as soon as he had Buck down at the end of the bar.

No, Hutton had not welshed. He had been surprised that the Pelton half of the old firm was still in business, but seeing it was, Hutton would see he got his share of freight. There would be enough for all. The mines at Ruby looked better with every foot of shaft and tunnel; it looked like another Comstock.

Only one thing had worried Hutton, and that was the prospect of being isolated by snow for a month to six weeks every year, maybe three months in bad years, and, when Buck insisted that he would be able to deliver every week regardless of snow by means of his own route, Hutton showed new interest. He would, in fact, be willing to pay a premium, say $20 per ton, on time freight during the winter, provided Pelton would guarantee a minimum delivery of 100 tons a week. Caution made Buck draw back from this, fearing a snow-slide or some other unforeseen occurrence, so they compromised on 200 tons each two-week period, Hutton guaranteeing this amount of freight, and Buck guaranteeing to deliver it. In addition, with only a momentary hesitation, Hutton wrote him an order against the express bank for $8,000, payment in full for the November minimum.

But now that the deal was closed, John was curiously alarmed. "We'll have to build that road and *keep* it built, keep it open, too. By gosh, I hope I made no mistakes. Say, whar we gitting wagons and stock?"

"That's my job. You build the road . . . you and your Pike's Peakers."

For wagons and stock, Buck sought a third partner in the enterprise — big, hunch-shouldered Frying Pan Murray, once of Denver, his father's competitor, now crowded out of the lucrative Benton-Last Chance traffic when the Circle J outfit established a monopoly on the Wolf Creek toll road. Murray, with his idle stock, would be willing to try anything.

John, in the meantime, rode to White Pine Valley. There were folks in that country that would hang him if they could, so he approached warily, across September-brown fields to the old fur-company buildings where most of the settlers were living, but only some kids and a dog took note of his approach.

He asked for the Widow Cobb, gave each of the kids a bitty nugget from his pocket, scratched the dog behind the ears, got rid of his chaw, and went to her door.

"Lord be praised!" cried the Widow Cobb, lifting both arms in a sign of blessed relief. She was a rangy, raw-boned woman and with the gesture her big, rough hands almost touched the ceiling. "It's him, it's him, it's the Comanche, he ain't been hung after all."

"I warn't born to git hung. I already told ye . . ."

"Oh, you're gaunt. Look at ye. You got no flesh on your bones. You been traveling with the wolf pack again. You strayed off the track of righteousness."

"I been washed by the blood and rectified by the spirit. I'm a pilgrim and weary, Sister Cobb."

"Set down." She pulled him to a chair. "Feel them arms. You're gaunt. I've seen jerky carcasses with more flab in their muscles than you got." She called one of the kids who was peeping inside. "Waldo, help this poor gentleman off with his boots. Now, you set, and I'll cook a snack for you."

John sat, moaning from luxury, his feet heisted, toes wiggling. "By grab, Sister Cobb, you'll spile me for heaven with this sort of treatment."

Stuffing wood in the fireplace, fanning it with her apron, she said: "I only hope you make it, Brother John."

"I just go down the trail o' life, helping men with their loads, and offen some of 'em I've lifted the gold, seeing that's the heaviest thing thar is in the world, heavier than lead even, and the ruination of more men than whiskey and chewing tobacco put together. Remember how the parson used to sing . . . 'Ye should help the weary pilgrim, ye should lift his heavy load'? "

"He didn't mean gold. He meant the *spiritual* load, not lifting things with the help of a Navy six."

" 'Seek not the treasures of this world for they do corrupt and destroy.' I tooken from the rich and gave to the poor." And to prove the point he sang, twitching his bare toes to keep time:

Now I sing of old Comanche John
And his partner, Whiskey Ike;
The only motto that they had
Was share and share alike;
They robbed the bank at Uniontown
And coaches three or four,
They robbed the rich-unrighteous
And they gave it to the poor.

The Widow had scant liking for the song. "What you need is a woman's care," she said. "You need to be mothered and patched and fatted up."

"Woman, I don't aim to wed until I made my mark in the world." She gave him such a stare he got his feet down and explained: "I'm in the freight business now. Yes, I am. Freight contract, wagons, stock, everything. All except a road. And that's whar you're going to help me. You and your Pike's Peakers. You're going to build road, trestle, and snowshed, and every man that builds will own his own stretch of road, and collect toll offen it, and make himself a bit of money."

"You mean abandon our farms, the farms we worked for and slaved for . . . ?"

"It won't hurt to abandon 'em for the winter. Unless you're too lazy. Unless ye'd all rather set the winter out in an easy chair."

"John, you know better'n that." She hung the kettle of congealed venison stew over the new fire and stood up to say: "If your offer's on the fair, then I accept it for 'em. I do, and I'll see to it ye get your workmen. You're right about sitting in a chair all winter, humping over a

40

fire, getting in a woman's way. By dang, if there's one thing I can't stand, it's a shiftless, chair-sitting, tobacco-chewing, whiskey-tippling, idle man!"

CHAPTER
FIVE

Sweat and Connivery

At night they got everyone together in the old trade room of the fort — eighteen men, their wives and larger children, a rough-garbed, work-hardened, discouraged group with scarcely a grubstake to show for their first year on the soil. They numbered only half of those who had settled the valley; the rest were gone to the greener country of Oregon, or to the gold fields, or to work for one of the freight lines.

Stocker, big and red-whiskered and stubborn as always, got to his feet and said: "We're not quitters. Not us. We're sticking to the White Pine, so don't try to paint any gaudy picture because we'll have none of it."

Big Betsy Cobb said: "I fought to keep us together just as hard as you have, and that's just why I called this meeting together. Brother John has got an idee that'll *let* us stick together, and give us the money we need. Winter work, and we can farm enough through the summer."

Stocker was truculent, but he sat down on a bench and listened. Others expected little to come of it, too, but John explained to them just how it was, drawing a map of the pass, telling about this stretch of proposed road and that, and how each would take a piece of it, some long and some short, depending on whether it was easy grade or hard, and build the road, after which it was his to charge toll on at a rate of twenty-five cents a ton during the snow, and ten cents at other times, and not just for one year, either, but ever and anon, until maybe a railroad came in — which would be never, over *these* mountains.

Young, red-headed, banjo-playing Rusty McCabe, who had a wife and an eight-month-old baby to think about, was the first to claim a share. Kippen, who was pulling stakes anyhow, was next, then Stott and his hulking, dull-appearing, teenage son Veltis. An argument ensued whether Veltis should be allotted a full share. It was left unsettled.

John asked for more volunteers. When none offered, Betsy Cobb arose and stormed at them, saying no worthless, loafing, tobacco-chewing man was going to clutter up *her* kitchen that winter, no, not by a crock full, because *she* was declaring *herself* in on the scheme and claiming herself a piece of road.

"What do you aim to do, build snowshed or blast rock?" Shallerbach hooted at her, and she answered: "Neither. You're all going to dig my road for me, because I'm going to feed ye and provide for ye, and have a warm place for ye when you're tired and sick and discouraged."

Stocker then said he would go, and then Shallerbach, Joey Nelson, and Artis Turner, while Voss said he would think it over. Voss, after talking to his wife, was on hand to sign up next day, and that evening George Nealy, who had gone prospecting the summer before, got wind of it and came in with two Chinese laborers and asked for a share.

John estimated that these, perhaps with the help of some of Murray's teamsters, could do the job. He did not care for Artis Turner, who would probably quit anyhow, and he'd disliked Ambrose Stocker ever since Stocker had wanted to hang him over on the Idaho side, but all in all it was a tolerable group.

It took a couple of days to get the outfits together, and then one more when Kippen and Shallerbach came over from Shako Gulch with a two-horse scraper that required some blacksmithing. Finally they set out, in wagons loaded with camp stuff and grain, the entire harvest for some of them, with extra horses, mules, and even a yoke of oxen coming up in a remuda under the charge of Veltis Stott.

The journey by road required four days. It was evening when they made the last weary pull through Stumptown to the grassy, *cirque*-like area they had chosen for the main camp. A tent was there, but it was empty, and a note was pinned to the flap signed by Buck Pelton saying he had gone to Benton to close the deal for the Frying Pan outfit and would be back Tuesday. Tuesday was the day before — Buck had been delayed.

Comanche John's farmers went to work cutting and skidding logs for shanties, and with that work under way he rode the high country up and back, first in a general reconnaissance, and next with a square and plumb-bob sighting outfit, surveying the road. After mapping it, he divided it into ten segments, some long and some short, depending on the terrain, and on the sheds and trestles that had to be built, later on. By then, the cabins were far enough along for shelter, and Buck was in from Fort Benton with the vanguard of the Frying Pan freight outfit.

"Where's Murray?" John asked, surveying the wheel-sprung wagons and the gaunt state of the mules.

Buck did not try to hide his fatigue or his disgust. "In Jackass, drunk."

Big Betsy Cobb came around to say: "I don't think we should be forming no partnerships with a drunken man."

John said: "Sister Cobb, just so his mules are sober, that's all I ask."

John offered to divide the road by lot, or he offered it to their compromise, except that the bottom stretch of half a mile belonged to the Widow Cobb, and that would have to be finished first, as a co-operative venture, in order to get supplies to the upper slope. They elected to choose after going over the ground with the result that Stocker took the long mile-and-a-quarter stretch up from the Widow Cobb's, with Kippen, Stott, and Shallerbach going third-shares on the three segments of grade and snowshed to follow; Nelson and Voss taking the next two; Rusty McCabe, who was good at axe work, taking a quarter-mile bridge and snowshed piece; George Nealy some steep grade and fill; Artis Turner, a whiner and procrastinator, after choosing and rejecting two other segments, finally settling on the 200-yard trestle because it was shortest.

45

This left a bit at the top which John had originally added to the trestle, but which they had decided to call half a share and give to Veltis Stott.

Back at camp, Buck was having his trouble with Murray's teamsters. Many of them had gone a month without pay, and without exception they took one look at the towering Chilkao and pronounced the whole project to be crazy. With nothing to do they spent what money they had on whiskey, and traded what they had for more, and all the while Murray was in Jackass City, as drunk as any of them.

Buck finally got Murray to camp and kept him locked up until he was sober. Murray emerged repentant. He needed a jug to sober up on, but when that was done, heaven be his judge, he was off the stuff for good. Murray just wished that somebody had a pledge so he could sign it. He stood outside, and said it in a loud voice so everybody in the clearing could hear him, yes, he was off liquor for good, and, if anybody found him drunk again, he just hoped they'd hit him with a shovel, and beat in his head with it, and then use it to dig a hole and bury him.

He got money from Buck to pay off his teamsters. It cost almost $900. Then he got more money for supplies, and rode away, straight past all the saloons and fancy houses in Jackass City, and he spent it, every cent, for stock feed from a French-Cree rancher on the Deer Lodge. And when he got back, he let everybody smell his breath and there was no taint of whiskey on it.

Murray's freight outfit, lying idle, was quickly eating its way through Buck's slender capital. Murray got a job hauling flour from the mill at Hell Gate. He put other wagons to hauling horn-silver ore from the Potosi Mine at Lucky Camp over to Fall Creek where two Mexicans had set up a *patio*. The Potosi owners were broke and paid off in corporate stock that John declared to be worthless, but which Buck took and sold at a 25% profit to a German in Ruby. Fifteen years later that same block of Potosi would have made him moderately wealthy, but of this Buck had no anticipation, and the $8.25 a share price elated everyone.

In the meantime, Betsy Cobb's section of switchback road was completed and the men moved on, each to his own section. Stocker, a Herculean laborer, with the help of a good team and plow, dug out his section of road, and shoveled and scraped it level, finishing it in eight days. Above him, Shallerbach, Stott, and Kippen had run into tough going through timber and slide rock around a bald-faced flank of mountain that time after time required drilling and blasting. Kippen decided to quit. He sold his shares to Stocker for five dollars and a saddle horse and departed for Last Chance.

Now with Stocker on the job, the tempo increased; he kept them going every daylight hour, and they worked by the light of pitch torches far into the night. Nelson and Voss made headway, and on the next piece McCabe had built a chute and had spent all his time getting out timbers and lagging for his snowsheds. He sold a horse and used the money to employ an Indian helper. As yet he had not built an inch of road, and as his segment was cut by a very deep gully, nothing more

47

than a pack horse could be taken to the sections farther up. Nealy and Turner complained bitterly of this state of affairs until Comanche John sent a crew of Murray's muleskinners and roustabouts above to put in a bridge, and dig out the main portions of the road.

At the very summit, Veltis Stott surprised everyone. Left to his own resources, with the others predicting that they would have to do the job for him, and it would teach him not to cut off a man's chew before he could spit, Veltis did what he could with hand tools, and then walked down the other side half a mile to the new shaft building of the L&M's Carlotta Mine, where he pointed out to the superintendent that his road could be used to advantage in bringing mine timbers in from the south side.

He then borrowed what he needed, a team and scraper one day, a load of giant powder next, and even a team of drillers when the Carlotta's shaft was flooded by a broken pump. As a result, he finished almost as soon as Stocker; then, refusing to work on the lower sections of road for just his board and keep, he got a job underground on the Carlotta's No. 2 tunnel working a muck stick at $6 a day.

It was now getting on toward November, and the road had to be finished. The lower three-fourths contained many bad stretches, but these could be fixed later on, even with snow on the ground. A try-out wagon, heavily loaded, had no trouble until it reached Nealy's where a sharp switchback held by cribbing and rock fill proved too narrow to swing the six-mule team and wagon, and had to be widened.

McCabe's snowsheds were still not built, although most of the timber was down, but they could wait. With luck, the heavy snow would not come until mid-December. With more luck they could even get by without snowsheds, for the deep accumulations could be trenched, and later the trenches covered over with poles, and then with new snow to make a tunnel. The thing really barring them was the trestle that Artis Turner had chosen to build because it was the shortest piece, and it looked to him like the easiest.

Turner had dug some footings and skidded about sixty pieces of timber. A series of misfortunes had befallen him, for he had cut his foot with an axe; he had been ill with the mountain complaint; his grub had been raided by skunks; one horse went lame, and, while tending to him, his other horse strayed. Out of grub, he went hunting, got lost, and wandered without food for two days.

The grub situation was particularly galling to Turner. Here were the others, most of them close enough so they could ride to the widow's for a hot meal a day, but here he was, left high and cold, with 10,000 skunks so he had to hang his grub by wires on the limbs of trees, and, furthermore, he had been shim-shammed into taking the poorest section of road, and nobody would lift a finger to help him; all the others had somebody to help *them* — a partner, or a couple of Chinamen, but not him. Why, even that Stott kid had some helping him, men bringing equipment over from the mines, and him so dumb he didn't know enough to pour water out of a wet boot. And when, in spite of his luck, he did get some timber out and start to place it, and build the trestle, who should come but that black-whiskered scoundrel named Smith, who really wasn't Smith at all, but a road agent, wanted by the law, to tell him he wasn't doing it right and would have to do it over. Well, Turner said, he'd show them a thing or two, all of them; he'd just sit there, and not lift a finger, and maybe they'd find out he was some important, after all.

A meeting was held at the cook house. At Stocker's suggestion, Turner's segment was declared forfeit, the others taking it on equal shares. Turner then rode away to Jackass City promising to "see someone", and they'd find out whether there was a law in the country, and whether they would take a man's property away from him, the same property he'd slaved his fingers to the bone for, because he had title, he had a paper signed by Buck Pelton, and it was a *deed*, according to law.

He saw a lawyer, Judge Harris, lately disbarred by the Oregon Legislature. Harris rode out and tacked up a notice signed by Ox Miller, president of the Jackass and Gold Run Miners' meeting, filled with ink blots and whereases, saying the road was closed by injunction. The road wasn't closed because wagons were running over it, and Comanche John, arriving that night, used the notice for target practice.

Anyhow, they had greater worries. Frying Pan Murray was drunk again; he had taken the payroll with him, and the muleskinners were threatening to quit.

One of the mules died. On the day following, another died, and, on the third, two more.

In Jackass City, word got to Murray that his mules were dying. He sobered enough to mount a horse and came out with a vet, or a man who said he was a vet, who thumped the bellies of the two that had just died and pronounced them dead of poison hemp. When it was pointed out that the plant was unknown in the mountainous locality, the vet looked superior and departed. Murray, beset by his unpaid teamsters, also made haste.

Poison hemp! Comanche John had a suspicion that guards would be useless. Hames probably had someone right in camp. So that night John posted himself uphill from the corrals, in the deep blackness of spruce timber, and made himself comfortable for a long vigil. There was no moon, but an edging of new snow around about made it light enough to see after a fashion. And he could hear. Comanche John had hearing like a prowling catamount's.

He waited minutes, and hours crept past. It was cold — below freezing, and he had little enough on. By grab, if he wedded the Widow Cobb, *if* he did, the first thing he'd have her make would be some red, hand-knit, woolen underwear, thick and scratchy, the kind you sewed yourself into and didn't come out of until April. John's present underwear was full of holes as a harness, and he didn't have socks, even — only long-cut strips of wool wrapped around his feet, mummy style, and they were always gee-hawing, making holes one place and lumps in another.

Suddenly he alerted himself. Someone was coming, and not up the trail from Jackass, but quietly, through the timber, on a deer track directly beneath him.

He waited — he waited for what seemed to be a long time, then he heard a low whistle. A shadow moved from behind the cook house — a silhouette, tall, with an easy shoulder movement that he recognized. It was Buck Pelton.

"Hello!" he heard Buck say in his husky, quiet voice.

A girl answered — Nettie Bowden.

They'd had it all planned to meet; they'd been meeting before; it was all plain to John now. It explained Buck's peculiar night absences, and the way of him when he came in, the drunk-without-liquor way of a man in love.

John chuckled to himself. "*Her*. And right from under Hames's nose."

They were in the darkness below him, and were talking quietly; he could hear the notes of their voices without catching any of their actual words. He wanted to hear — not because he was snoopy, but just because he wanted to. So he got closer, sliding down through soft, damp forest cover in time to hear her say that she was certain of it, that her father and Hames were buying Murray out.

"Murray can't sell," Buck said. "We own two-thirds of his outfit."

She said: "All I'm telling you is what I heard Dad say. Murray is selling. They're closing the deal day after tomorrow."

"Why are they waiting?"

"He wants cash. Hames has to wait for his payroll to come up from Salt Lake."

"Where's Murray now?"

"I don't know."

"We'll have to find him."

They moved away, still talking. John knew that they wouldn't find Murray. It was too late to do anything about Murray. Hames would see to *that*. Hames would have Murray well under cover.

CHAPTER
SIX

The Way it should be Done!

Comanche John had a plan of his own. He put up a snack without disturbing Betsy Cobb and rode off, down the gulch and across the ridge, southward. At dawn he was at the creek where he had first met Buck Pelton.

What a coach robber that lad was, he ruminated. *No training. Breed is dying out, getting hung. Trains taking over the old routes. Trains . . . there's the real death of the coach robber.*

By grab, if there was one thing Comanche John despised it was a banging, clanging, stinking train. That was one reason he had headed into Montana. They'd never get a train into that territory, that was a certainty, and, if they *did*, they'd never get it back out again.

The sun warmed him. He was in no hurry. He had all day and most of the next. He napped on a hillside. He rode on, past Bentley's, and got ready to spend the night in the open, building a small lean-to by notching spruce saplings and bending them over and weighting their tips with rocks. It was snug underneath on a bed of boughs, with the soft twigs of the saplings billowing over him. By grab, this was fine. This was really living.

He lay, thinking more about railroads, and how they would ruin the country. Well, the railroads would come, but they'd go again, yes, they would, after their usefulness was spent, after the mines were worked out and there was no more payload for them to haul. He'd listened to the speeches down in Colorado about how the railroad would bring in the farmers, and how the farm things would keep the rails humming, lifting themselves by their own bootstraps, the weakness of it being who'd buy the farm stuff after the gold was gone? What'd they pay for it with? With more farm stuff, or with engine smoke? Oh, yes, sir, John had listened to a lot of big talk in his day, but most of it didn't stand up to the clear thinking of a man out under the stars beneath a spruce lean-to!

In the morning he reached Brass Kettle Creek. He was out of the mountains now, on a sagebrush flat between hills. He sighted a bridge. That was the spot he'd figured on. He watched a freight outfit move from sight. It left the flat empty as far as his eye could see.

He inspected the bridge. It was made of heavy logs laid crosswise to traffic resting on even heavier logs set in the opposite banks. Traffic had worn down the approaches on both sides, leaving deep holes in the gumbo earth that had been filled in with stones — a rough job.

He removed some stones. He did not take out all of them, just enough to make a hole that would loosen the coach driver's teeth when he hit it, but not enough to stop his vehicle entirely. He decided to mask himself, fixing a kerchief beneath the band of his hat so it could be pulled down when needed. He left his gunpowder pony back in the bushes, reins around the saddle horn, so he could follow. After that, there was nothing to do but wait. In half an hour he sighted the dust drift of the approaching coach.

He got down and crouched ankle deep in the creek, with cold water slowly finding its way through the seams of his jackboots. Around the projecting end logs of the bridge he could see without being seen.

He wondered if Bill Eads would be riding shotgun again. He hoped it *would* be Eads, for the fun of it, although it would be better if Eads didn't know he was in the country.

Well, it *was* Eads, sitting, long and limber, beside the driver, swaying with the coach, that same rifle between his bony knees. The coach slowed not a quarter-wheel turn as it careened toward the bridge. He had a brief view of the undersides of hoofs and the bellies of horses, then the wheels hit with a bang that loosened every dowel and joint in the coach.

The driver cursed. The rear wheels dropped and came up again. The coach lurched almost off the bridge. Comanche John pulled himself up, slowed by his water-filled boots, paused at a crouch. The side of the coach was over him; people were there; they could have looked down and seen him; they could have touched him, but the unexpected impact was like being belted over the skull. They weren't in condition to see anyone. The rear wheel barely missed him. He stood and grabbed the luggage carrier, pulled himself up, climbed to the hurricane.

The driver, standing, was filling the air with curses for the "sodbusters and punkin-rollers" who he blamed for the state of the bridge. Eads sat tight, clutching the iron seat rail, apparently still a trifle groggy from the impact.

John, on hands and knees, pulled the kerchief over his face. He drew his right-hand Navy and said: "Covered!"

He spoke softly so his voice would not be heard inside the coach, but it reached the driver and the guard, and they stiffened to its tone.

"No, don't look around. Keep your eyes on the road and your minds on staying alive."

"Where the devil did *you* come from?" shouted the driver.

"I be first cousin to the eagle and brother to the hawk, but don't ask me the secrets of my clan. The point is, I'm robbing this stagecoach. I'm after the Hames payroll. It's here. It was put aboard in Salt Lake, and, if ye want to know the exact amount, I could give ye that, too."

He said all this, trying to disguise his voice, but he had an idea that it was recognized by Eads, who sat with his shoulders pulled in, high and narrow, looking straight ahead, the rifle still clamped between his knees. A bandage around his right forearm was a reminder of that other encounter, but he could use the hand; he was using it to grip the barrel of the rifle.

John poked his Navy against Bill Eads's spine. "Git up."

He did so, straightening his legs, propping himself with the backs of his legs against the seat.

"Loosen your gun belt . . . Thar. Let it fall . . . Good. That's first-rate. That's top riffle. I can see ye been robbed before. Know better'n to cause trouble when you're up ag'in' a man that knows his business. Just let the rifle go. It'll lean. Step over it . . . Thar. That's fine. By grab, you've mastered the art of staying alive in the wild Nor'west. Now turn, face the outside, jump!"

For the first time, Eads hesitated, and for the first time he looked. John anticipated that, and anticipated the dive that he might make for him, but Eads didn't have the chance, for John's right jackboot shot out, catching him in the belly, doubling him, sending him sprawling to the ground in waist-high sagebrush.

The dry sage raised a billow of gray dust as the coach rolled on.

"Man overboard!" a passenger bellowed, leaning out of the window, trying to get the driver's attention. "Hey, somebody fell off the top."

"Don't answer," said Comanche John.

The passenger leaned farther out and kept shouting and pointing at Eads who by now was on his feet, just standing there, watching.

"You lost a man overboard!"

The passenger stopped suddenly, as he looked down the muzzle of Comanche John's Navy.

"It was his destination," John said politely, "but this be a scheduled coach, and wayside passengers git off on the fly. Regylations. And don't go to yawping ag'in' 'em or I'll punch your ticket for ye, and I'll do it with a

Thirty-Six-caliber hole, and I'll do it without you taking it out of your breast pocket."

That settled that. John heard no more from inside the coach. He settled back. He enjoyed the ride, chewing, looking at the scenery which actually wasn't so much, only the sage- and jack-pine-covered hills with roundish, heaped-up lava rocks forming some narrows out ahead. That would be the place — the narrows. He could stop there, and wait for his horse, and keep watch both ways, and in case of trouble he could fight off a whole posse.

He propped his boots up to let some of the water run out; he even hummed a tune, but not the Comanche John tune, for it might have hinted who he was.

"Well?" cried the driver, stiff at the edge of the seat.

"No hurry. We'll heave-to in the rocks. I'll stay fixed and you dump off the money chest."

He was keeping watch of the driver without seeming to, and a slight movement of the fellow's mouth told him something. Of course, it wouldn't be the main strongbox — Hames would know better. Hames would be too foxy.

"The *private* chest. The small one, the hid one." John noted with satisfaction that he'd hit on it. He chuckled. "Ye shouldn't think to fool me. Didn't I tell ye it was aboard? And *whar* it'd *come* aboard? Might be no end to the things I know. I want Hames's private pay money, no more, no less, and it'd be unhealthy to try to trick me."

The driver was very jittery. "I'll not try to trick you." John knew that he wouldn't.

They stopped amid red-brown rocks that radiated the heat of the midday sun, and the driver, crawling across the hurricane, reached in the boot and got out a plain satchel. It was locked, so John slit the leather with his Bowie, reached in, and inspected the packets of money. Union money, those down-and-out greenbacks, the kind you should spend fast before old Robbie Lee took Washington and started stabling his horses in the Supreme Court and put the government printing office to making handbills for all the runaway slaves that the Abolitionists had spirited away from the honest property owners of the South.

It amazed him that Frying Pan Murray would want this sort of stuff in payment for the mules and wagons of his freight line. Well, he wouldn't get it, not this money, because John had it. He drew the money out, a packet at a time, and stuffed it inside his shirt, cinching up his belt so it wouldn't leak out down his pant legs. Finished, he climbed to one of the out-jutting rocks.

"Now git," he said. "Drive and keep driving."

Half an hour later the pony was there, coming at John's whistle to get a handful of brown sugar, and, mounted, he rode back toward Jackass.

CHAPTER
SEVEN

To Arms, Stumptown!

He arrived late. A crowd was on the street, most of them gathered near Judge Harris's law office, so he guessed that the coach had arrived, the robbery had been reported, and the miners' meeting had convened.

He left the street, descending to the safety of the deep placer cut. The sluices — miles of dripping plank troughs — tonight ran clear water with everyone, even the Chinese laborers, up listening to the speeches. Somebody was saying that somebody ought to build a gallows, and build it *now*, so it'd be ready, because Comanche John would be up there, at the freight camp, on the other side of Stumptown, and they ought to burn it out, and hang some of the others, too, because it was a nest of thieves, and anybody but a fool could see it was a blind, that freight road, over country so steep it'd maroon a goat, and snow so deep later on you couldn't dogpull a toboggan over it.

Then another man got up to have his say. He was in favor of hanging Comanche John, but talk wouldn't do it. No, it was his suggestion that they *catch* Comanche John first and hang him afterward. That didn't set well, and others started to heckle him, and that made him mad. He was red-freckled and red-headed and undersize, and the kind who got *really* mad. Yes, he shouted back at them, he'd been in Idaho and knew about the Comanche, all the places they'd *claimed* to have hanged him, or *tried* to hang him, and, if they *did* catch him, they'd better hang him with a rough rope, because he had the slipperiest Adam's apple this side of Pike County, Missouri, and, when they got him hung, they'd better cement him in his grave, and roll down eighteen ton of rocks on his chest, and then not brag a word for ten days and ten nights because the old Comanche was the type that wriggled through a small hole.

Yipee! thought John, slapping the legs of his homespuns, *that's me, I'm a ring-tailed ripper from the Rawhide Mountains, and I'm harder to hold than the weasel that fell in the soap bucket.*

Ox Miller then charged back to the platform, braying about the honor of Montana Territory. "Ladies and gentlemen," Ox said, although the only ladies present were some of the girls leaning from the second-story windows of the New Orleans dance hall across the street. "Ladies and gentlemen, I speak to you of the honor of the territory and of Jackass City, the future hub of transportation of the entire Northwest, and especially of the man who is putting her there, Mister Lawford Hames, and how he's been robbed and victimized and driven to the end of his patience, and how something should ought to be done about it. Well, I say, something will be done about it. We'll go up there to that den of thieves called Stumptown, and *get*

Comanche John, and *hang* him, and, as for me, I'm willing to do it as a civic deed, and no thought to the reward. Yes, as for the money I'm willing to contribute my share to the city, and it can be used to buy things to enhance the town . . . gas lights on iron posts, and a water system, and a fire engine, and a monument to George Washington, the father of our country . . ."

"Hold on, Ox," somebody shouted, "how much ree-ward they got up for that road agent?"

"Plenty. Here, and I-dee-ho, and Californy . . . just plenty. And I say we should write letters this very night informing 'em we've *hung* Comanche John, and the rewards are due and payable as of this date, and, if they try to renege, they'll be sued."

Such foolishness was too much for Comanche John's stomach, so he rode on, staying to the shadows until he saw the lights of Stumptown.

Stumptown looked nothing like it had a month or two before. In anticipation of its future eminence as the jumping-off place to Windigo Pass, it had grown from its first clutch of cabins to a town of 200, with a dozen keg-and-tin-cup saloons, a couple of stores, and a dance hall with a temporary canvas roof. Tonight everyone was awake. They saw him coming and word of his arrival raced along the street.

John stopped as Fred Bentloss, the storekeeper, town-site promoter, and unofficial mayor of the town, came toward him.

"You have your crust, Smith, riding up here like this with all that ruckus going on in Jackass. Did you know they intend to hang you? You'll get us all in trouble."

"I do feel sorry for ye," John said with poor temper, getting one leg around the bulge of his saddle for comfort. "I'll tell ye something else they plan on, and that's burning ye out, all of ye, the whole damn' town, can't ye *see*? I'm Comanche John, that's their talk, and *why*? What's the real reason? I'll tell ye . . . to give 'em an excuse, wreck the town, wreck the road, make Jackass City the freight hub instead of Stumptown."

This put a new light on it. "They're not burning my place down!" one of the saloonkeepers bellowed. "I got three hundred dollars invested in my place and they'll be plenty of Jackassers carrying bullet lead before *I* let 'em set fire to it."

Someone else said he'd been there, and he'd heard talk about burning the town, that Ox Miller himself had called it a den of thieves.

Stumptown was really excited now, arming and barricading itself. Bentloss tried to take command, but before he could bring any sort of order a boy rode from the direction of Jackass, quirting his pony, shouting: "They're coming, they're coming, there must be five hundred of 'em!"

Five hundred there might have been, but fortunately at least four out of five had just come to see the hanging. Ox Miller, tramping along in the lead, drew up when he saw the log barricade they'd hastily thrown across the road.

"Stand back!" Bentloss called out. "You're not burning Stumptown."

A gun cracked, adding point to his words. Ox dived for cover and the men behind him scattered. Someone from the Jackass crowd fired back, and then guns let go from everywhere.

When things quieted, they could hear Ox, bellowing: "Bentloss! Hear me, Bentloss, you're taking responsibility for sheltering an outlaw!"

"You're not burning us out."

"We got no idea of burning ye out."

But the firing commenced again. Ox retreated among his men, recognizing the futility of argument. Dawn came, gray at first, and then with a touch of color around the high peaks. With daylight, it was all over. The only casualty was Lou Haffey, owner of the Michigan Saloon, who lay on his pine bar with a bullet through both legs. As for Comanche John, he had long since ridden to Betsy Cobb's for breakfast.

CHAPTER
EIGHT

A Deadfall, by Grab!

"Lank," Betsy Cobb muttered, pouring and frying. "Hungry as a ranging wolf. You been on a wolf's business, too, more'n likely."

Talking from the only part of his mouth not full, Comanche John said: "I been out on company business o' confidential nature, Sister Cobb, convincing Frying Pan Murray he shouldn't sell out to Hames."

Buck Pelton came through the door behind him, and asked: "How did you know about Murray and Hames?"

"I be an old woolly wolf. I sniff things in the air."

Buck laughed and sat down across from him and watched him load his mouth with fried pork and griddle cakes. "I hear that Hames can't raise the money."

"Saddened to hear it. Whar is Murray now?"

"I don't know."

"Under lock, I'll wager, or kept too drunk to move. So be it. Hames is welcome to him. If thar's one thing the Widda Cobb and me can't stand, it's a whiskey-drinking man."

John insisted on paying all the teamsters double wages. He was very free with greenbacks. Dissatisfied with progress on the trestle, he hired men at half again more than the prevailing wage.

On the third day after the Battle of Stumptown, he awoke to find a blizzard licking around the mountain, drifting snow across McCabe's uncompleted snowshed, but the work went on, with men quitting and John raising wages to get them on again, for it was November, and the first 200 tons of contract time freight would be due in Ruby by the 15th.

"We'll make it," Comanche John said, coming down from the pass after a day and a night without sleep, stamping wet snow on the widow's floor, rubbing his ears that were discolored from the cold. "We'll git the freight over. By the way, whar *is* the freight?"

Buck was seeing about the freight. It was piling up at the Willard & Sankey warehouse in Jackass City, but Ox Miller, with fifty blank warrants, was waiting to arrest the first Stumptown rebel who came to claim it.

Buck returned, having succeeded in escaping arrest, and rode straight on over the pass to see the London & Montana people about it. He returned with a note from Hutton, addressed to Willard & Sankey, threatening to terminate all company business with that firm, whereupon the resident manager bustled around among the Jackass City business concerns, pulling enough strings to get Ox to rescind his order, and the first wagons were loaded without incident.

And they were waiting for the trestle to be finished. Temporary plank, laid across, allowed the passage of an empty wagon. That night, by torchlight, the first four payload wagons started up the pass. It still snowed, but crews went ahead, keeping the way cleared. By morning they were at Nealy's, where a dirt slide held them up. It was cleared, and they rolled on, beneath snowsheds, roofed with half-round lagging, and already, in places, drifted over, forming tunnels. The trestle workmen catching sight of them came to meet them. Someone led a cheer: "Hip-hip-hooray!"

In the midst of this, no one paid any attention to the three men who were walking across the trestle from the Ruby side. Each of these carried a brace of Navies, and the big fellow in the lead had a sawed-off double shotgun for good measure.

Dillworth was shouting — "Get back to pegging plank and stop hootin' your heads off!" — but, when the first workman started back, he found himself stopped against the muzzle of the double shotgun.

"No, you don't," the man said, and he meant it. The man was Moose Petley.

Stocker cried, "What goes on here?" and drew up, recognizing him. "Why, you're Moose Petley!"

"Yes, you're damn' right I'm Moose Petley, and, no, you didn't kill me on the Big Hole . . . *murder* me, I should say, ingratitude if I ever seen it, after the way I fought your Injuns and showed you the trail. Well, you're on the other side of the gun today, and this is legal, because I'm *Deppity* Petley, duty sworn."

"What do you want?"

"I got a writ of attachment for this bridge."

"Who from?"

Moose, getting the sawed-off with an elbow and one hand, drew a paper from the pocket of his curly-buffalo coat and, holding it upside down, announced: "Whereas and to wit, this section of road, bein' known as the Sky-High Trestle, belonging truly to Artis Turner, a freeholdin' citizen of this republic, is hereby seized and appropriated for the benefit of him and his heirs forever."

"Who signed it?" a man jeered. "Was it Lawford Hames, or that San Francisco millionaire that's backing him?"

"The judge signed it. There's his name."

Nealy had come up around the crowd, against the inner bank where, for a distance, the road had been blasted from the mountainside. In his hands was a newfangled German needle-fire rifle. He stepped out, away from the others, surprising Moose with the aimed gun.

"Now, git or you're a dead man!" Nealy shouted.

A gun cracked from above, and Nealy went down, head and shoulder first, across the steep side of the road. He slid for ten or twelve feet, and might have gone over the cliff farther down, but he was caught by jack spruce and juniper, and there he lay, apparently not breathing.

For the space of one or two seconds everyone seemed stunned by the shot. Then they milled, looking for cover. The cry of — "Ambush!" — went up. A puff of gunsmoke hung over stunted spruce at the rim of the cliff.

Someone fired from the road. A bullet hit rock and screeched. There were more shots from above. One of the workmen fell, and got up and ran, bent and staggering, and fell, and got up again, and someone grabbed him and dragged him to cover.

Moose Petley and his two companions were momentarily forgotten, and they lost no time getting down off the trestle. They were beneath, sliding the steep rock, using pilings and brace timbers to check their descent, and for protection, too.

"Get Nealy!" Stott cried, and, when no one moved, he went himself, pushing away those who tried to stop him.

Stott was all by himself in the road. A bullet whanged down, showering stone and snow between his boots. He flattened himself against the cut-away bank and shouted: "Moose, stop your guns, let me get that wounded man! Where's your Christian mercy?"

Moose answered: "I'll show Nealy the same brand of Christian mercy he'd have shown me if we hadn't got him first."

Nealy, in the meantime, had shaken off bullet shock and rolled over. He got to hands and knees. He crawled up to the road. One of the ambushers above inched out to fire on him. Shallerbach, who by this time had reached a commanding and protected position some yards uphill, poked his old .50-caliber Jager rifle over a log, aimed, and pulled the trigger, all in one movement. The ambusher was hit; he fired wildly; the impact of the Jager slug knocked him over on his back; he had enough left to spring to his feet, then his legs buckled, and he gave the impression of springing head foremost over the edge, falling to the trestle, and off that, ending among slide boulders almost at Moose Petley's feet.

"Get 'em, go get 'em!" Moose was bellowing. "Blow 'em back to Stumptown!" he shouted without once showing so much as a sleeve of his curly-buffalo coat.

Stott in the meantime had dragged Nealy to cover. He was not badly hurt. Other rifles from above drove the road builders back, first to the protection of Nealy's bridge, and then to a snowshed. From there, some of them doubled back along the mountain. Both sides looked up, with neither in actual control of the trestle.

It was evening when word of the battle reached Comanche John in Stumptown. He went from saloon to cabin to barbershop, trying to raise a force of men, but he found only three who would join him, and one of those was a boy of fifteen who was soon dragged home by an irate mother. John then looked for Buck Pelton. Someone had seen him walking to Betsy Cobb's. Betsy was alone and in such a state as John had never before seen her.

"She'll kill him, she'll kill him," Betsy was saying.

"Who'll kill who? Sit down, woman, and stop waving that old horse pistol. Who'll kill who?"

"That girl, she was here with a gun, and it was cocked, and it was loaded. Do you think I'd let her threaten him if it hadn't been . . ."

"What girl? Nettie Bowden?"

Betsy cried: "She's the one, that vixen, that devil . . ."

"*Her*? That pretty, sweet . . ."

"She's a young devil with skirts on," said Betsy. "She's incarnate. The Good Book warns us of her kind."

He couldn't believe it. "She was after Buck with a gun?"

"She walked him out of here at the point of a pistol, with the hammer drawn back, and not three minutes ago. Oh, I been in a state. I didn't know what to do. Buck told me to sit right here, or . . ."

"What'd she want?"

"Claimed we had her paw, old Bowden, a prisoner, a hostage, that old moneybags, that wicked old San Francisco skinflint . . ."

"Whar'd they go?"

"How do I know? Toward Jackass, I suppose."

"Afoot?"

"Horseback. It's four mile . . . o' course they're horseback."

Comanche John rode off at a gallop, through Stumptown, down the freight road, among the cabins that were interspersed with clumps of timber where one settlement frayed out to meet the other.

It was dark here, with only an occasional cabin window to light his way. The houses became more numerous. This was Jackass City. He would have to move more carefully. Behind him, a man in a cabin door stood with a blue-flaming match. It gave him a start, the quick burst of its flame, like the flame of gunpowder, but the man was only lighting his pipe.

He was close onto the Jackass business district and about ready to turn back when he looked up a steep street terminating against a cut bank, and there they were.

"Ho, thar!" he said.

She recognized him. He saw the blued shine of gun metal in her hand. She tried to watch both ways and was plainly at a loss where to point the gun.

"I mean ye no harm," said Comanche John. "And you're wrong about the lad, too." He took off his black slouch hat and held it over his breast in a posture of sincerity. "We got no idee what could have happened to your paw."

She cried: "Perhaps you'll tell me I'm wrong when I say you used the information *he* got from me" — she pointed to Buck — "and used it to intercept the Hames payroll. That was the start of Dad's trouble . . ."

"Buck had nothing to do with robbing that coach. I robbed it myself. It was my own idee. I was uphill that very night, hearing every word ye said. So he didn't abuse your confidence. But, as for holding your paw a hostage, why that ain't our style."

"I have a letter signed by you . . ."

"By *me?* Gal, I can't even read and write, except for the things wrote on a pack of playing cyards, and that's the handwriting of the devil, I been told."

She had already put the gun down. It was plain that she was relieved to have Buck Pelton absolved from blame — she was so relieved that she had no ire left for Comanche John. "Oh, Buck!" she said, almost in tears.

He turned his horse and rode close to her; they sat so close that their knees touched; he put an arm around her.

He said: "Now tell me what happened . . . what really happened."

"I think they had a quarrel . . . Dad and Hames. It was about the mules, and some other things. I think Dad threatened to pull out of the partnership. It would have broken Hames. He needs money. He claimed the L & M was holding back on their freight, thinking they could get it over your road cheaper. Then Dad disappeared. I just didn't see him any more. I tried to get Ox Miller to look for him. He did . . . for a while. Then Hames said that Dad was being held prisoner in Stumptown. He said he had a ransom note from Comanche John."

The gunpowder roan moved, and now he had his head up. Comanche John became alert. He turned, and started back down the trail. He watched for movement; he listened. He was slouched, his shoulders loose, his hands hanging beneath the outthrust butts of his Navies. He hummed a little tune, and spat tobacco juice at the top of a stump.

He could see only the black shadows of cabins, and of pines, and the soft phosphorescence of snow up the mountain.

"Ho-hum," yawned John, so he could be heard at some distance, "reckon I'll ride on to the hotel for a drop of civilized likker."

He had no intention of riding to the hotel. Once on the road he intended to hit for Stumptown at a gallop, but he did not get to the road; a shadow disengaged itself from the shadow of a hut. He kept riding. There were other men, and there was a shine of guns in their hands.

"Halt!" a voice said. "Move and we'll sink ye with lead."

By reflex John had drawn his Navies. He stopped without lifting them. There were men ahead and at both sides and behind. It was a deadfall, and he had ridden into it. *She had led him into it* — that was his first thought. Only how could she, not knowing he would follow? Then he remembered the flame. It was a signal; it was all set up; they had been waiting for this, waiting to grab him the first time he ventured to set foot in Jackass City.

CHAPTER
NINE

A Warning for the Young

Comanche John opened his hands and let his Navies fall. The guns struck with scarcely a sound on the damp forest cover. He kept riding at a slow jog, saying: "Why, gent'men, what sort o' celebration ye got fixed up for me?"

"It's him!" The voice belonged to Ox Miller. "It's the Comanche. Now, watch for trouble. He'll make a break for it."

"Not me," John said. "I aim to live for a year or three."

"You won't live for an hour." That was Bill Eads. He could see Bill, tall and loose, a gun in each hand.

Miller said: "Get his guns. You, Eads, on that side, and Cary, you . . ."

John said: "Ye got me wrong, boys. I carry no metal. It's ag'in' my religion."

The two men walked up, cautiously, and felt for his pistols. "Clean," Cary said. "Holsters empty."

"Look in his saddle leather."

"He's clean, I tell you."

Buck Pelton came riding down but was kept away by their leveled guns.

"Stay clear, lad," John said. And, when Buck commenced to talk roughly to Ox Miller: "No, git home!"

"Don't let him go to Stumptown . . . he'll get a crew together."

"Let him!" Eads said grimly. "Nothing I'd rather have than some of those Stumptown scalps on my saddle."

They bound John's hands in front of him, each wrist with tight wrappings of rope with a swivel knot in the saddle so he was able, handcuff-style, to manage his horse.

"Tie his legs, too," Ox said.

Cary answered: "Oh, hell, Ox, there's no point being an idiot. They'll laugh at us, bringing him in like a Ee-gyptian mummy."

Ox surrendered the point, but he still didn't like it; he had heard too many stories about John's previous escapes — about him getting away with a rope still around his neck, and how he'd been buried, but too tough to die, and had been dug up, in the middle of the night, by his Arapaho sweetheart, but, of course, that one was just plain foolish.

Eads said: "He's all right. I hope he does try to escape." He pressed the cold muzzle of a pistol to the skin back of John's left ear. "I only hope he does try it!"

Ox said all right, but they'd better get him to town, no telling what those renegades at Stumptown'll try. They'd better get him in, and try him, and convict him, and hang him.

"Bless you," said John, "I know ye wouldn't hang me without full benefit of the law. And I know ye won't hang me without the supplications of a minister of my own faith, either."

"Where is he?"

"In Hell Gate."

"That's two days' ride," a man said.

"Not with a good horse."

Cary said: "We'll give you till midnight . . . if you're lucky."

They were getting their horses, from sheds, from the timber, from below in the placer cut, but no more than a few were gone at once, and always three or four guns were kept aimed at him.

By now, word of his capture had raced along the gulch. Men were in doorways calling it to their neighbors. A foot crowd formed; others hurried to join them. A tall man, very pop-eyed and bumpy of face, had carried a torch up from the head box of a sluice, and, when they started toward Main Street, he placed himself in the lead.

"They got him . . . they hanging him tonight . . . it's Comanche John!" he shouted.

"They hung him two year ago in Californy and I seen the corpse!" someone called.

A boy of twelve or thirteen competed with him, beating a tin pan, shouting: "It's the Comanche . . . they caught the Comanche!"

It soon developed into a full-blown parade with pans beating and men keeping time saying — "Hip! Hip! Hip-Hup-Hip!" — as they marched. A drunken teamster, standing on the high seat of a wagon, was singing in a wild, nasal tenor:

> Have ye heard of old Comanche John
> Who robbed the Yuba mail,
> And left his private graveyards
> All along the Bannack trail?
> Then gather 'round ye teamsters,
> And listen unto me,
> Whilst I sing of that old varmint
> The fastest gun thar be.
> John had four boon companions
> All loyal and all true.
> Thar was Three-Gun Bob and Dillon
> Big Mac and Jake-the-Jew . . ."

They were past then, and his voice was drowned out. "Get a rope!" someone shouted. Someone else shouted it, and in a few seconds everyone was shouting it. Standing on the log wall of a half-finished building a man was calling: "Hang him here! Hang him on my premises! I'll pay a hundred dollars spot cash, to charity, if you hang him on my roof tree."

"By grab," said John without being heard by anyone, "I never knew I was so popular."

"Hundred dollars to *what* charity?" Ox asked.

"To the widows and orphans of the Union Army."

"Make it two hundred."

"Two hundred it is."

The lumpy-faced man, still with his torch, headed into the roofless building. "Make way, make way!"

Someone had a rope. It was tossed over the ridgepole. A knot was tied.

"Get a bar'l."

"We don't need a bar'l. We'll hang him off his horse."

John, who found his time shortening unexpectedly, cried: "Hold on, what sort of small-skate camp is this ye got hyar? Don't I git a trial?"

"You already had a trial."

This was a new voice. It was Hames's. He had come in the building by the rear and now stood beneath the swinging rope. He stood with his feet set, hands on hips, broad and powerful. He did not have his pistol concealed tonight, nor did he carry a small pistol as on their first meeting — he had an Army .44 strapped around the outside of his coat. The butt of his old bullwhip, however, projected from the right side pocket.

"I warn't here," said John. "How could ye hold a trial?"

"You don't need to be here. You were tried and convicted."

"By you, Hames? I knew ye owned the camp, bragged about owning it. Own the town, and the miners' association, and Ox Miller thar is just your errand boy."

"You won't start a quarrel here," Hames barked, obviously afraid that he might. "We're agreed on one thing, and that's the right medicine for a road agent."

A few in the crowd said he should have a trial, but most of them wanted to see a hanging, and they mobbed in, pushing the horses of the prisoner and his captors across the corduroy walk to the open-roofed buildings.

"Every man deserves a word in his own behalf!" shouted John.

Cary stopped against the push of the crowd and succeeded in swinging his horse around, making room. "By damn, yes!" he said. He used his gun to drive back the crowd. "I say *yes*, give him a chance to have his say."

"You gone crazy?" asked Bill Eads. "Let's hang him before he talks his way out of it."

"Even a Chinyman deserves to have his say."

"He's going to talk, he's going to talk," the word was repeated. "Comanche John's going to make a speech."

Ox Miller thought about it, and decided *yes*, he should at least have a chance to say something. Ox stood in the stirrups, cupped his hands, and bawled out: "He's goin' to talk. Hear ye, he'll git quiet to have his say if we have to wait till sunup."

The voices died down. John cleared his throat and waited. He waited until the last talker had stopped and it was so quiet he could hear the running boots of late-comers thudding the sidewalks.

"Ladies and gent'men," he started. "I stand before ye a guilty man."

"He admits it!" someone whooped.

He waited again for quiet.

"Yes, I admit to it. I been a road agent for twenty year, my soul is black with sin, and my hands with gunpowder. I been wicked to shame Gomorrah. Behold before ye a man that could have been something if he

81

hadn't taken the wrong road. And look at him now. Boots on his feet what leak the snow. No socks, just wrappings of flannel. Homespun pants with the knees busted out, no underwear even."

"You won't need warm clothes where you're going, John."

"That's true," he said to the man. "I won't, because the oil in my lamp o' righteousness is mighty low. That's why I wanted to talk, so I could warn the young, tell 'em not to follow the trail I did. Don't carry more'n one gun. Avoid strong drink and bad companions. But if ye *must* rob, do it proper, military style, and never spend a poke in the same county ye got it in. That's how I operated, and, though I'm a goner tonight, I lasted many a mile more'n most road agents. Yes, I did, and I drop a tear when I think of 'em, all the brave lads. Jimmy Dale, Three-Gun Bob, Whiskey Anderson, and a heap more, all under the sod, hyar, I-dee-ho, Coloraydo, Calyforny." He sat, digging at his whiskers with brown fingers on which, by the torchlight, his nails looked white as pieces of chalk. "Plenty o' gold I took, but I never had the chance to enjoy it. Never even had a chance to spend it."

"What happened to it?" This was the fateful question, but John made no sign that it was.

"I'd tell ye, yes, I would. I'd tell ye whar to git it, only it'd do ye no good. Be the ruination of ye, like of me. Gold is the root of evil, it's the trunk and branch, too, and it's the apple that blooms on the tree."

A short, thick-bodied man pushed in close as he could and said: "It's *my* gold if it came off the Bentley coach in June."

"The Bentley coach!" John hung his head. "I can't look ye in the eye for shame, but I must confess it war me that robbed that coach."

"What'd you do with my gold?"

"Wait." He lifted a hand for quiet. "All in due time. I hold nothing back. I'm in a mood to confess. I robbed that coach. I did, and the one in August, too, and I robbed the bullion wagon from Brass Kettle Creek. I forgot the date . . . and the coach to Last Chance at Cliffrock Station. Then thar was the strongbox at Mauch Gulch, and the Bannack coach at Badger Pass on June eleventh, and the retort amalgam from Silver Bow, and I lost *that* in a faro game."

John went on, enumerating this robbery and that, confessing to all the ones he'd heard about, and he made some up, and finally he stopped, and said even that wasn't all, that he'd forgotten some, and was sorry for it, but his memory wasn't what it used to be.

"You got all *that* and still don't have money for underwear?" asked Cary.

"Alas, it's the truth. I didn't dare spend the gold. Dee-tectives made it too dangerous. Every shipment assayed, tested, known for this gulch and that by its nature, they'd have caught me. But I had an idee." He looked all around as if afraid some outsider from Ruby or Last Chance might overhear, and said, lowering his voice and making the crowd hold its breath to hear him, "I *took* that gold, and brought it *here*, and dumped it, of night, in the tailings of the mines. Just at certain places, of course, known to me, marked in my mind. I figured I'd come back when the gulch was washed up, everybody moved on, and stake the old ground, and mine it over again. That way I'd been in the clear, legitimate mining man, a millionaire. But I'll be hung and beyond mining, ever."

A dozen men were now demanding to know exactly which tailings had been salted. Then two of them got to jangling and almost came to blows over the right to certain tailings heaps, one claiming them because they originated on his claim, the other because he had the ground they were dumped on.

"I paid you seventy-five ounces of gold for the privilege of dumping on your poor-scratch hardpan claim," the one cried in a fury, "and those tails are mine, I own 'em! I'll fight for 'em. I'll sue you through every court in the territory."

Ox Miller got them apart, and said: "We'll settle it in miners' court. Anyhow, what makes you think he picked *your* tailings? Center of town, too dangerous, he wouldn't go thar. More'n likely he went down the gulch and dumped it in mine."

"Ask *him*."

"Yes, where did you dump it?"

"Not all in one place," said John.

"But where . . . what places?"

"I did it here and thar, by landmark. I'd have to hunt."

"Show us!" they all started shouting.

"Why, I'd be pleased," said John. "I would, ordinarily, only it's dark now. I'd have to wait till morning, and now I'm all confessed, and well, damn it, I'd sort of had my mind set on gitting hung."

Hames climbed to the unfinished log wall and, holding with one hand, shouted down through the other: "He's lying . . . he's hid no gold . . . he's stalling for time!"

"Well enough for *you* to talk," he was answered. "You got no claim, you don't stand to lose, all you care about is getting shot of a freight competitor."

"That's a lie."

"Tell me to my face it's a lie."

"I am telling it to your face."

Ox Miller didn't know what to do. He knew it was a ten-to-one chance that John was lying, but there was that *one* chance, and damn it, he owned some tailings, too.

He rode back and forth, trying to keep the crowd away, saying: "We'll call a miners' meeting. We'll put it to a vote."

The lumpy-faced man had wedged his torch down between two segments of the corduroy so he could use both hands to gesture with while engaging in the dispute. Comanche John let them jostle him closer to that torch. It was there, so close his pony twitched from the heat of it on his side. He unstirruped his boot and held it out, the edge of the sole in the flame. It was hot on his toes, but he kept wiggling them, and he stood it until his boot sole commenced to smolder.

No one paid the least attention to him. They were still arguing. He pulled his foot back, all slowly, casually, without looking, and touched the burning leather to the side of his horse.

The gunpowder moved as though stung by a bee. He had no room to run, so he went off the ground at a sunfishing leap, and John allowed himself to be catapulted over his head to the space between the walk and the hitch rack.

There was Ox Miller on the other side of the hitch rack, fighting his big gray horse with a stiff bridle rein. Comanche John climbed to the rail, balanced himself for a second, and leap-frogged across the gray horse's rump. He was in the saddle, wedged behind Ox. Ox was shouting — "What the hell?" — and John got his tied hands over his head, around him.

Ox fought; his strength would have freed him, were it not for the ropes on John's wrists, but these held him like a hoop around a barrel.

"Ya-hoo!" said Comanche John, "what say to a gallop?"

Ox cursed him and ripped from side to side, almost dumping both of them to the ground. John's hands located a Navy. He managed to draw it. He turned it inward and pressed the barrel to Ox's stomach.

"Got ye covered!"

"You'll never get away," said Ox, his abdomen stiff at feel of the gun.

"Pull your Bowie!"

"What?"

"Bowie!"

Ox drew the knife.

"Blade out."

Ox did that, too, and John, working the rope up once and down once, cut it, and his hands were free.

As the rope parted, Ox was freed, too. He came around with an elbow aimed at the side of John's head, but John, grasping Ox's other Navy, was already over the side.

"Thar he is!" cried Ox. "He's yonder by the hitch rack!"

Comanche John seized the torch and hurled it as far as he could. He took a long step as a bullet tore slivers from the walk between his feet. He was against the unfinished wall as a second bullet thudded deeply into a log.

"Hyar I am, come git me!" he whooped. "I'm half horse and half alligator and the other half of me is horned frog, too tough to eat and too ornery to die."

He climbed and vaulted the wall. The swinging noose almost hit him in the face. Bill Eads, a loose-jointed scarecrow with a gun in each hand, rose to meet him, but John hit him with a blast from his left-hand Navy, dropping him in his tracks.

"Whoop-a-raw!" he bellowed. He paused briefly against the wall. "I'm a ring-tailed ripper from the Rawhide Mountains and I've kilt more men than the seven years' plague."

He crawled through one of the side window holes. He dropped to damp earth on hands and knees. He crawled. He got up and ran, following a narrow passage between the unfinished building and a saloon next door. He could have gone on, up a zigzag path that climbed an almost perpendicular bank to the next street, but they would expect him to do that.

He crossed at the rear of the building and went in the back door of a saloon. The place was empty. He stopped to help himself to a pound of flat-plug chewing tobacco, and ran to the walk. There he mingled with the crowd, staying clear of the wavering torchlight.

He could hear Ox Miller's voice: "Git back, block off the street. Wait for him to come out."

The crowd was not so thick as John had hoped. Too many had run for cover. No kidney for a fight. Damned bunch of Yankees and pumpkin-rollers. By grab, that amount of shooting wouldn't have scared an old-time 'Forty-Niner crowd very far. Country was taming down, getting soft. He crossed the street, cursing the country and all the people in it.

He was safe for a few seconds in the shadow of a wooden awning, against a rain barrel. Ox was getting his men spread out, and he didn't like it. It was a dirty way to play the game, that waiting in ambush instead of rip-roaring after him on a horse.

He had to lie low. He climbed the rain barrel, reached above, found the wooden rain trough, used it to pull himself to the awning.

He hoped he could stay there, but it was too narrow. He rested on one knee, against the false front, and looked at people on the street below him. He could have reached down and touched their hats.

He stayed close against the building for shadow, spat on his hands so they would stick better, reached around to the roof, propped himself, crawled to it. He climbed to the gable, praying that nobody would look from one of the hotel windows and see him, and slid down.

He could not see where he was jumping, but he jumped. He lit in ashes and bottles that clanked and crashed. No one paid any attention. No one was here, in this alleyway. He had three chances — to go down the alley, to try to make it to the placer cut, or go inside Hames's big Overland Hotel.

Said I was going to the Overland, didn't I? Told 'em that up yonder when they captured me. So that's whar I'll be.

He walked through the side entrance of the hotel. He was in a hall filled with the smell of cooking. The hall led to the kitchen and the dining room. He wasn't hungry. He came to some narrow stairs, climbed to the second story. He listened to a man's hurried walk along the hall. He didn't want to be recognized, and perhaps have to shoot.

He tried the nearest door. It was locked. The voice made him stop and come back. He knew who it was — it was Bowden, the old gentleman, Nettie's father.

He rammed the door with his foot, and the lock gave way, tearing free of the soft pine casing. He was in a dimly lighted room with the arch to a second room beyond. He closed the door, and stood listening while the footsteps grew close.

"Who is it?" Bowden asked.

"Hush."

The feet went past without pausing. John went to the draped archway.

"Be ye alone?"

"Yes."

He used the barrel of a Navy to lift the drape. The old man was in bed, very pale, fumbling, trying to get up.

John bent over and looked under the bed; he checked on the window to make sure he couldn't be seen from the street below.

"You!" Bowden said, recognizing him.

"And an improvement on the company ye *been* keeping, I'll wager."

"What was all that shooting? What's happened?"

"Why, they took it in their heads to hang a man, but he was reluctant."

Bowden had made it to his feet. He stood, holding to the bedpost. His legs, where they could be seen below his nightgown, were thin as the lower legs of a chicken. Or maybe they could be likened to the lower legs of a grouse — that was how blue they were.

"We have to get out of here," whispered Bowden, "while he's gone."

"Whilst who's gone?"

"Ed Gaw. He was guarding me. He left when the shooting started, but he'll be . . ."

"He was holding ye prisoner? For Hames?"

"Yes, but hurry."

"By dang, I'm hurrying for no Ed Gaw." John was content to rest a while, give things a chance to cool off. He sat down, tilted his chair back, and put his boots on the bed. "You let your Ed Gaw come if he wants. I'll care for him. Besides, ye got no pants on."

90

There were no clothes in the room. They waited for Ed Gaw. He was there ten minutes later, a red-faced, stupid-looking man. Finding the latch broken, he stood holding the key, and stared sag-mouthed into the muzzle of the heavy Colt in John's hand.

"Git out of your pants," said John. "The gentleman wants to wear 'em."

They left Gaw gagged and tied to the bed. They could hear drinking in the hotel bar, but the rest of the building was quiet, and it was quiet outside. They probably could have left by the front way, but they didn't. They went around back, and up a side street.

"Only bad thing," said John, watching for pursuit and seeing none, "I lost my horse, but he'll come home, maybe he's home now. And my guns. Got to find my favorite Navies."

"But my daughter . . ."

"She'll be yonder." He had to help Bowden along; at times, he practically carried him, and it was hard going. "Five to one we'll find her in Stumptown."

CHAPTER
TEN

No Body for the Hearse

Nettie was at Betsy Cobb's. She was almost as relieved to see John as she was her father, for she hadn't led John into a trap, that is, not intentionally, and she told him so over and over.

"Take care of your paw," John said. "For land sakes, gal, how could ye lead me into a trap when ye had no idee I'd be following?"

She helped Betsy Cobb put her father to bed, then they gave him hot tea and rum until he recovered from an attack of the shakes.

Bowden's first words were addressed to Buck Pelton, who came in while this was going on.

"What are you doing here?" he asked.

Nettie moved over beside the young man, took his hand, and said: "Dad, we're going to get married."

Bowden lay, looking at them, letting the rum take effect. "I didn't mean that. I mean . . . why isn't he up on the pass . . . fighting to save his road? Hames is hauling powder up there by pack horse. He'll blow your trestle to toothpicks. I knew that . . . that's why he was holding me prisoner, so I couldn't warn you."

Comanche John and Buck Pelton sent for horses and rode off in the early dawn, through intermittent snow. Occasionally, at a distance, they heard the crack of gunfire. At McCabe's first snowshed they met one of the workers coming down, and he told them that the trestle was safe enough, that it still was not controlled by either side, and it was certain that Hames's bunch could not plant powder under it.

"The old gentleman dreamed it up," Buck said, reassured, after his first look at the trestle. "It would be suicide trying to carry powder in there . . . we'd shoot them like ducks in a pond."

From a vantage point on the road they watched the fight, if it could be called that — with guns at such long range a man had to arch his bullet ten degrees. To John's experienced eyes, however, a lot of the shooting from Hames's side seemed to be just that, shooting for the sake of shooting, to hear a gun go *bang*.

John decided to climb for a look at a new angle. He rode by himself through several rocky turnings. No road here, only a deer trail. The pass was off to his left, a V-shaped passage between peaks that towered 1,000 feet higher on either side. The shooting, although farther off, seemed closer than before because of his elevation and because of the cliff faces that reflected the sound.

He had to leave his horse behind. He clambered over huge rocks at the base of a cliff. He crawled among windfall logs and waded snow to his waist. After a half hour of this, his legs aching from fatigue, he rounded a flank of the mountain and looked across a precipitous slope close to the summit, smooth and bare of trees, scarred by snow and earth slides of other seasons. Below, he could see several stretches of the road, tiny from distance, but not the trestle — it was obscured by the steeper drop of the cliff. In the other direction, up the slope, lay an accumulation of earth, small rock, and snow. Above this was the summit — a knob of solid granite.

The accumulation had been undercut and left precariously in place by the snow and earth slides of other years, and, as he watched, he saw the movements of men and pack animals near the point of the V. There, a rough pillar of granite projected through, its key point, its anchor.

They were preparing to blast it. He could not tell how far the job had progressed. It would take him an hour to go below, and summon help, and argue with them, and convince them, and then get back, and an hour would certainly be too long.

He decided to go on by himself. The damned Pike's Peakers got in his way anyhow! One certain thing, however, he couldn't approach directly across the slope. They would be able to see him and knock him off with a rifle bullet, and anyhow it was too steep, the footing too slippery and friable. He would have to go around.

He retraced his steps, climbed in the protection of the mountain flank, and reached a place of about equal elevation. This time, when he came around, he had the protection of a dike of rock, a porphyry more resistant to erosion than the rest of the mountain, and hence left to form an uneven reef at most places three or four feet above the surface.

He walked, he crawled, sometimes on hands and knees and sometimes on his stomach, and at last, as the wall commenced to play out, he came up for a look. He took off his hat and very carefully got his eye to a crevice. He was now only a long pistol shot away, and he could tell who they were and what they were about.

Three men were unloading a pack mule, doing it very carefully, wary of the explosive they were handling. A fourth man directed them. That was Moose Petley. A fifth stood look-out above the pillar where they were preparing the blast. That was Hames himself. Two other men, who he had seen from below, had apparently gone around the summit, leading the unloaded mules.

John decided to move just a trifle closer. There was little dike left, at times none at all, but he crawled on his stomach, managing to keep concealed in the large slide rock. To quiet his nerves he muttered to himself: "What an idee! Rock slide, accident. Wipe out maybe eighth mile o' road. Whole trestle, too. And men. Whatever luck gave 'em. That's why their men were staying clear, far off, making no move to *take* the trestle. But ye can't tell about a slide. It might jump and do no harm at all. Now, down in Coloraydo . . ."

Down in Colorado John had seen some mighty stupendous snowslides. Whole mountains shedding their skins. This wouldn't compare with *them*, but it could be bad enough. He was so close he could hear the crunch of their boots in rocks, he could hear them grunting, saying a few words when need be, mostly saving their breaths.

He peeped again. Moose Petley, still in that curly-buffalo coat, was standing almost atop him, but his side was turned, he was pointing to put this can of powder there, and the other one there, and string the fuse out.

John quietly drew a Navy. Then he cried: "Up your hands! Make a move and you're a dead man!"

A can of powder was dropped. A gun crashed from above. That was Hames. The bullet hit close to his cheek. It powdered rock and stung him. He dived to a new place, came up with the muzzle of a Navy through a break in the rock, and fired back, but Hames had fallen to his belly.

"Stay where you are!" Hames was shouting. "He's alone. There's just one man!"

Someone cried: "Stay and git blasted to Jericho by powder? I'm clearin' out of here."

Hames cursed him and tried to kill him as he ran. He moved along the knob and fired at the spot where John had been. The bullet glanced away with a hornet sound.

"Moose, set the fuse!"

John no longer knew where Moose was.

"He's alone, I tell you, I'll keep him down!" called Hames.

Moose answered: "*I'll* keep him down, *you* set the fuse."

It was quiet. John did not know which had decided to touch the fuse, and which had a gun ready to kill him when he showed himself.

He had to move to a new spot. He did it by lying flat on his stomach, boots spread, and pushing himself with first one elbow, and then the other. There were three rocks, forming a little nest. He could get to one knee there without them seeing him. He did it.

A trickle of dirt was flowing from above. It had been loosened by a man's weight. John guessed at the source of the trickle and raised a trifle. He looked, but no one was there.

"Moose!" shouted Hames.

Hames fired and the bullet flattened itself against one of the boulders. At the same instant he saw Moose Petley — on the wrong side.

For a fragment of time John looked down the round, black muzzle of Moose Petley's gun. He let himself fall as the gun roared. He was aware of the flame bursting in his face. He felt the sting of burned powder and wadding. Concussion deafened him and seemed to blow the whole side of his head away.

He rolled over. He acted without thinking. There was a solid place under his feet. He stood and saw Moose and he fired both pistols.

The discharge of his guns and of Moose Petley's guns came in a sudden, almost instantaneous roar. But Moose was hit, and his bullets flew over John's head.

Moose went down. He slid, boots out, his eyes stunned and off-focus. He rolled over and over and kept rolling for 100 yards down the slope before a mass of snow-filled brush stopped him, and he lay there, doubled and still. So he was finished — like he should have been on the Big Hole.

John watched him while trying to guess where Hames could be. He might have run for it, only Hames wasn't the running kind. A sound came to his ears — the rasping sound that a hobnail makes on stone. It could have come from this way, or that. It's hard to be certain of direction among the bare rock faces on a mountain.

He raised tentatively, and a bullet hit rock three inches from the crown of his hat. He deliberately drew a second shot, and a third. Each came from a different angle, so he knew that Hames was going around the crag toward the powder charge. He would split the fuse short as he could, and run for it, and leave John below to be caught in the resulting blast and avalanche.

John drew another shot. The next was not a shot — it was the empty *click* of a hammer. Hames's gun was empty, or it might not have been. It could have been a trick, and an old one. John couldn't take the chance, and he couldn't afford *not* to take the chance. He decided to go farther along the reef, then suddenly up and over it, and then everything would be in the open. But at that instant he heard the hiss of the fuse.

He got to his feet. Hames was up there, just splitting a second fuse — the make-sure fuse in case the first one missed fire. John had him against the muzzle of his guns. He could have killed him. There was only one little thing. Hames was in a nest of powder, and the bullet that killed him would have gone on through and set the blast. So John did not pull the trigger, and Hames, still crouched, turned and grinned down on him.

"Covered!" John said. "Git that fuse. Pull it!"

Hames laughed at him. He laughed like he really thought it was funny. "Go ahead and shoot," Hames jeered.

"Damn ye, pull the fuse!"

Hames kept laughing. It had a high-pitched, crazy sound. His gun was at his feet. It was empty, or he'd have had it in his hand. But he was safe from John's Navies, and he knew it. "Come on!" he said, thrusting his hands out. "I don't need a gun. I can handle you with these."

Comanche John kept climbing, judging the distance between them as the fuse burned with a red hiss and black trail of smoke and as its flame disappeared among the cans of powder leaving a twisty, smoldering ribbon of black ash behind it.

Suddenly Hames moved. He bent double, and for an instant John thought he had lost his nerve and was making a grab for the fuse. But he didn't. He came up, with the coiled whip drawn from somewhere inside his short sheepskin coat.

He tried to swing it, to wrap the lash around Comanche John's neck. John went to his knees and felt the cut of it over him. He came up again, at a crouch; he lunged up the last few feet of slope, thinking not so much of Hames as of the fuse, and that he had to reach it.

A Bowie flashed. He seized Hames's wrist. They went down together and fought across the rocks. Lying on his side, feet spread wide to brace himself, John reached with his free hand for the fuse. He felt the scorch of burning powder. He almost had it. He tried again, but in doing it he had to move his legs, and that gave Hames the chance to spin him over.

Hames almost had him with the Bowie. John let go, twisted from beneath him, and the Bowie missed. He tried to roll over, to use his weight to drive the weapon free of Hames's hand. But Hames was too quick. He rolled at the same instant, and John, falling on him, landed on his doubled legs. The legs uncoiled and John was hurled backward.

John managed to land on his feet. He backpedaled, trying to gain balance on the steep slope. His body outraced his legs. He fell and rolled over and over and hit the porphyry reef that a minute before had been his protection from bullets. It stopped him. He lay halfway across it, trying to get his breath. He was briefly aware of Hames above him, clambering around the face of the crag, trying to reach safety farther up. Then explosion hit. It was like a blow from a sledge.

He was unconscious for perhaps a second. He felt thunder around him. He had no sensation of direction, of up or down. He lay on his stomach, hat under his face, arms around his head as rocks thudded all around. It seemed to last a long time. The thunder faded away. His ears stopped ringing. He gathered his thoughts.

He was still alive. He kept saying over and over that he was still alive. He opened his eyes. At last he was able to see. He sat up. There was sky above and earth below. The dike was still there and he was clinging to it.

The dike had saved him. It had protected him from the explosion and turned the avalanche that followed it.

Above him, everything was changed. The crag was gone, blasted away. Above it, all the tons of earth and rock were gone. Hames was gone. He had been right atop the explosion. Only dust and the smell of powder remained. He looked below, and saw the path the slide had taken — a reddish streak through the snow.

Yes, it was like the Gypsy gal had told him. He wasn't fated to hang, or get killed, but to die in bed, with his boots off, and his guns hung on the bedpost. He rested, and got his bearings, and finally he went below, and caught his horse, and rode around to see what had happened to the road.

Upflung strata of a resistant quartzite rock had deflected the slide somewhat, channeling it down through that same old cut where Nealy had had all his trouble, and the road was gone for a distance, but it wasn't bad, only a couple days more of building.

He could hear a lot of distant talking and shouting back and forth. Someone had been killed. He went closer to learn who it was. Smith had been killed. Smith — why, that was he.

Comanche John thought about it. It gave him a good, free feeling not to worry about hang ropes, or have the responsibility of being a big businessman, a freight line operator. He rode off by himself and took notice of what a fine day it was for November, and how blue the sky was, especially toward the north, in the land of the Blackfeet.

He tried out a chaw of the store tobacco. He spent the day at his ease, slowly descending, and at dark he had made up his mind.

There was a light in the widow's cabin, and Stocker's wagon was hitched in front. They'd be talking, Stocker and his missus and the widow, and that always created plenty of noise, so there was nothing preventing him slipping into the back door for just a snack. He got inside without incident.

It was dark, with only a little light coming over the three-quarters partition that divided the house, and he sort of smelled his way, finding some cold hardpan bread, a piece of jerked venison, tea, a string of some of the widow's secret-recipe smoked trout, and he found a pan to do some cooking in. He took an old blanket, too, and rolled his things in it, making a wolf pack. Then he was ready to go, but the widow mentioned his name, so he listened.

". . . and he was standing there, right by the bootjack, few more'n twelve hours ago, and I talked sharp to him about tracking his wet jackboots all over my floor. And those were my last words to him. Oh, I wish I could take those words back, but I can't . . . no, I'll never get a chance in this world."

Why, said John to himself, *the poor woman's crying.*

Mrs. Stocker said: "Now don't you chide yourself, Sister Cobb, a woman's got to talk that way to her men folk."

"I drove him out, and it war for the last time. And the way he *looked* at me, with that peculiar smile on his face, sort of far away, as if he could see into the future, as if he *knowed*. Like he had inner sight. Things like that happen, you know. It comes to folks in a flash. And now he's dead and cold and I'll never see him any more."

Comanche John wiped a tear from the corner of his eye.

"No," the widow was saying, "I'll never see him this side o' Beulah Land. When I think of him cut down in his prime, in the flower of his manhood . . ."

Stocker said: "I'd say he was a mite gone to seed."

"In the flower of his manhood! Who are *you* to talk ag'in' him, *you* that wanted to hang him over at Big Hole?"

Comanche John did a dance, whacking his pant legs silently, whispering: "Give it to him, Widow!"

"Don't you talk ag'in' my John. It may be he used strong language betimes, and he scratched, though why I never determined, and I suspected him of strong drink, but he was religious. Yes, I do believe he was saved."

John was tempted to step out from behind that partition and gladden her heart as it had never been gladdened before. But she was talking and he decided to wait for just a moment . . .

"Anyhow, he had bad habits because he lacked advantages. Well, I'd have given him advantages. I'd have broke him of chewing and scratching and cursing and all the rest, I would. I'd have done it with kindness, and, if that didn't work, I'd have beaten 'em out of him with the stove tongs. I'd have got him shaved, and dressed up, and you wouldn't have known him."

103

Comanche John decided not to gladden her, after all. He picked up the wolf pack with one hand and groped for the door with the other. He could hear her saying: "I do wish you'd see if you couldn't get a hearse here from Last Chance. I know it'd be expensive, but I think we should do it. And plumes. It would soften the blow if we had plumes. And see if you can't find the body. Laws, what good's a hearse without the body? Yes, you must find it, we *can't* have a respectable funeral without the body. I got my mind so set on . . ."

Comanche John softly closed the door. His gunpowder pony was in the corral like he hoped he'd be. And his old saddle. All was quiet, no watchman, only the teamsters drinking trade liquor and arguing over a game of seven-up. He rode down the gulch and across a ridge, and the last light of Stumptown was gone from sight, but below, to his left, he could see the road that led to New York Bar, and the Three Forks, and Confederate Gulch, and the Hooraw Diggings, and after that the wild land of the Blackfeet.

He breathed deeply, and took off his slouch hat, and let the wind blow through his tangled long hair. "That woman," he muttered. "I'm going to stay clear of that woman. She always *did* want to bury me."

He felt better with a mile between them, and better still with two, and at three he was singing:

Co-man-che John was a highwayman,
He came from County Pike,
And the only motto that he had
Was share and share alike.

The yaller gold came easy,
And he spent it just as free.
He always chawed tobacker
Wherever he might be.

The Feminine Touch

William Hickory Gupsworth was fifty-nine or thereabouts, and for the past twenty of those years he had done pretty much the same thing every morning — he had arisen at sunup, fried sourdough flapjacks and salt pork, and he had climbed the barren side of Wilsail Mountain to the portal of his mine, the U.S. Mint. But this morning was different.

This morning Gupp did not lie abed until such an hour as sunup. He was out of his bed before the sun was even a rosy streak above the horizon. He swept out his log cabin, blackened those parts of the Prospector's Friend cook stove that were commonly visible, and dusted the ore specimens along the windowsills. Then, carefully strapping the old straight-edge razor that Teddy Roosevelt had given him with his own hands, he shaved off a four-day growth of whiskers, leaving his face smooth and pinkish.

"Ah!" said Gupp, looking at himself in the oblong of rusty mirror that was fastened with bent-over nails above the wash dish. There was no doubt that he could pass for forty-nine. He might even pass for forty. But forty-nine was what he'd said in the letter and forty-nine was what it would be!

By the time he had tallowed his boots and donned his new green and red flannel shirt it was breakfast time. He built a quick fire of sagebrush stalks, fried his usual pancakes and salt pork, and started to eat. Then he stopped. He laughed and talked to himself out loud, the way so many solitary men get to doing.

"Well, by jingos, this has gone and changed my life already. Here if I didn't forget all about Herschel."

He smeared a pancake with sorghum, rolled it around a strip of salt pork, and, getting down from his chair a little, whistled a chorus of "Buffalo Gals". Soon, obedient to the sound, there came a rustling through some dry stuff beneath the cabin floor and a sleek, well-fed pack rat emerged through one of the broken boards. He waited until Gupp put down the food, then he scurried up and sat like a squirrel with his chin moving up and down, munching it.

"Well, this is the day, the one I been telling you of," Gupp said. He sounded pleased, chuckling and chewing all at the same time. "Didn't come close onto me this morning, did you, Herschel? Might' nigh didn't know me, shaved and slicked this way. Well, a man shouldn't let himself get run over at the boot heels. Sign of getting old. Oldness and lonesomeness. But the lonesomeness is all over now."

Gupp, first wiping the salt pork off his fingers on the dishtowel, went to the cupboard and tenderly got down a photograph. He leaned it against a table leg on the floor where Herschel could see. It was a woman of thirty or so holding a plump boy with ringlets.

110

"There she is, Herschel. The future Missus Gupsworth and child. Oh, this'll be a fine place for that boy to grow up. Plenty of fresh air, plenty sunshine, plenty hills to climb. I been thinking some of buying him a pony and cart when he's old enough to drive. Animals, that's what a boy needs. Oh, you'll have great times with him, Herschel. It'll change our lives some, but it'll be all for the best."

The woman was Mrs. Josephine Fedwick, who Gupp had contacted through the Pike's Peak Home and Happiness Society in Denver. Two weeks ago their correspondence had culminated in a proposal of marriage from Gupp and a prompt acceptance from Mrs. Fedwick, then a letter from Gupp enclosing $22 railroad fare, and now she and her son were due to arrive in Galena City on the Limited that very afternoon.

Herschel finished his meal and departed, leaving some pancake crumbs which Gupp carefully swept through the hole in the floor. He tidied the breakfast things and went outside to look at the sun. He guessed it to be eight o'clock so he had plenty of time to hitch Dolly, his mule, and drive the buggy down to Galena. He had just started out with a currycomb to get the burrs out of Dolly's tail when he heard the scrape and rattle of coach wheels and knew it was Steve Kegg, making his daily round trip to Whitetail, a slowly crumbling mining camp eight miles farther back in the hills.

Gupp listened, expecting the stage to roll on, but this morning its sounds grew steadily until it came into view

111

across the uphill hump of sage, juniper, and buffalo grass to Gupp's cabin. It was the mud wagon, drawn by two span of mules, with Steve in the driver's seat and some bags of Mormon spuds roped to the hurricane behind him.

Generally Steve loaded the freight inside on the floor and in the seats, letting the passengers, when there were any, ride outside as best they could, but today things had changed — the freight was on top and inside were a man and woman.

Steve brought his outfit around, lurching over rocks and gopher mounds to Gupp's cabin, where he dribbled tobacco juice discreetly over the side, wiped his whiskers on the back of his hand, and said: "Gupp, this yere lady and her boy blew in this morning on the skidoo and I guess maybe you was expecting 'em."

Gupp's circulation halted momentarily at his first glimpse of her. She was and she wasn't the woman in the picture. The woman in the picture was slim and old-fashioned while this one was horsy and middle-aged. And this was no baby boy with her, but instead a hulking fellow of twenty-one with pale eyes and a flat, obstinate face.

"What say?" said Gupp, stalling for time.

"Of course, he's expecting us," the woman said with an aggressive grasp of the situation. She gave Gupp a determined smile. "You *are* Mister Gupsworth?"

Gupp did not deny it. He retreated a little as the woman emerged through the coach door stern first, pawing one oversize leg for the ground. The boy

112

followed and the old mud wagon groaned to be rid of them.

The woman turned, giggled with a faded girlishness, and got her hat to better position on her head. It was a purple hat with pink plumes.

"I'm Josephine," she said. "You know . . . *Josie*. You always called me Josie in your letters." When Gupp merely stared at her, she said: "Well, I must say, Mister Gupsworth, you don't seem to be splitting yourself to make us welcome."

"Guess I was surprised," Gupp managed to say. "You were younger in your picture."

"Oh, *that*. I told you it wasn't a real recent picture, remember?"

"But the little boy . . . ?"

"Teddy *has* grown a bit, hasn't he? But boys will be boys. And now, Mister Gupsworth, if you will lend a hand with the luggage? There's my bags, and Teddy's trunk, and a box of things that the storekeeper sent."

Gupp wrestled the things from inside and from the boot. While he was getting his breath, Steve Kegg said: "That'll be four dollars' fare. The lad said you'd pay."

Gupp gave him the four silver dollars and stood, helpless to stop the coach as it rolled away toward Whitetail. Mrs. Fedwick had gone inside the cabin to sniff around. When he started to follow her, he was blocked by Teddy who towered over him with his shoulders thrown back.

"What do you do for amusement around here?" Teddy asked.

"Amusement?"

"Yes, the light fantastic."

"Well, mostly I just work in the mine."

"What mine?"

"Why, up the hill yonder."

"That there?" Teddy studied it. "Why, that's just a hole in the hill with some broken rock heaped in front of it."

"What the blazes did you think a mine looked like?" Gupp snapped, wanting to get inside where the woman was hauling stuff out of the cupboards. He had his assay chemicals there, the lead carbonate and potassium cyanide where they'd be sure and not get mixed up with the baking powder, and he wanted to show her how things had to be. "Maybe you think I should've dug the mine inside out so you could look at it stretched out on the ground."

"Mister Gupsworth!" Josephine said, standing straight with the baking powder in one hand and the cyanide in the other. "Well, now, is that any way to speak to your stepson?"

"Why'd he ask so many foolish questions?"

"The only way a boy can learn is by asking questions. Anyway, you'd better be careful how you talk to Teddy. He's stronger than he looks. Bend a horseshoe for him, Teddy."

Teddy looked around and said: "Get me one, will you?"

"Give me those cans," Gupp said, grabbing the baking powder and cyanide.

Teddy said: "I took the course in muscular development from Lionel Strongfort."

Gupp was trying to remember which can was which. He knew then it was the old, battered one. He carried them back to the cupboard.

"Now, this one," he said, "has to go here, and this one has to go there. Otherwise likely you'll have an accident."

"I know baking powder when I see it," said Mrs. Fedwick.

"That's just the point, this one ain't baking powder."

"What is it?"

"Cyanide."

Mrs. Fedwick screamed, grabbed both cans, and ran out the door with them. She came back wiping her hands on her dress.

"What'd you do that for?" asked Gupp. "That was my assay stuff."

"I'll not have poison in my cupboard."

"But you always know it . . . it's in the old can."

"Not . . . in . . . my . . . cupboard," said Mrs. Fedwick, drawing out the words.

Teddy said: "All I could tear up was one pack of cards before I took the course, but now I can tear up two. How many packs can you tear up?"

Gupp said: "I don't know. I never tried." He rescued the cyanide and carried it to the shed that was built over his forge and anvil.

Mrs. Fedwick said to Gupp: "And now you can put that big box of groceries in here on the floor."

Gupp had a hard time struggling it inside. He had never seen so many groceries in his life. Getting it over the step would have been too much for him had not

Teddy stood at a distance, telling him to pull it this way and that.

"*Whew!*" said Gupp. "It looks like we're going to eat mighty fancy."

Mrs. Fedwick had now sniffed in all the corners, including the tiny bedroom. She said: "Well, Mister Gupsworth, you said in your letters not to expect a mansion and I must say that we didn't find one."

"She's small but she's snug," Gupp said defensively.

"Well, I guess it will have to serve until you can build another one."

"Now hold on . . ."

"Surely you didn't intend this for a permanent arrangement." She looked back inside the bedroom. "We'll fix that up for Teddy. He can put his pennants on that wall, his exercisers over there, and I suppose there'll be room for his rowing machine if we buy a smaller bed." Mrs. Fedwick took a big breath. "Well, I guess I'd better get my working things on. Up to a new wife to be useful, I say."

Gupp was lifting groceries from the packing case. "What's this?" he asked, shaking a red and white box.

"Bran flakes," said Teddy.

"I eat oatmeal."

"The storekeeper wanted to send oatmeal, but we had him send flakes. Oatmeal ain't fortified. It's gone out. Old-fashioned. In the big cities everybody eats flakes these days."

Gupp didn't say anything. He dug deeper into the box, lifting out prepared waffle flour, prepared biscuit mix, prepared gingerbread mix, cans of ripe olives.

116

Mrs. Fedwick said: "Now, if you'll move those old tools, I think I'll put my clothes right there. Will you bring my suitcases in so I can unpack?"

Gupp thought of something and said: "You ain't aiming to just stay?"

"Well, now! If that isn't . . ."

"But we ain't married."

"Oh, that!" She laughed in relief. "That's all been taken care of. When I was in town, I saw that Gospel John person, and he promised to drive out tonight and marry us."

She listened to a *crunch-crunch* sound emerging from the grocery carton. She tiptoed over and peered inside. Then she screamed.

"A rat! An awful rat!"

The broom was handy. She tipped the carton over, frightened the rat into flight, swung the broom high. It came down, but Gupp deflected it.

"Hold on!" said Gupp. "That's Herschel!"

Mrs. Fedwick brushed Gupp aside and pursued the fleeing rodent around the house, swinging the broom, but he made the hole in the floor and disappeared.

"I hate rats," said Mrs. Fedwick.

"Well," said Gupp, "I always say they's good and bad in everything. I've known some mules I wouldn't've sold for wolf bait, but I don't take that as an excuse to go around killing all the mules I see. Now a rat, if you get to know him . . ."

"Me, get to know a rat?"

"Well, just for the sake of argument, say . . ."

"I got better things to do than argue about a silly thing like that. If there's anything I detest, it's a filthy, sneaking rat. Are you much troubled by them, Mister Gupsworth?"

"No'm."

"Well, I'll have this one before many hours are spent. I do wish I'd have put in a trap. I don't suppose you have a trap here. Well, I'll keep the broom handy."

"Just a stray, likely. If you forget about him, I'll mend that hole in the floor and . . ."

"A rat'll stay wherever there's food. Only way is to kill them."

"I'll get a club, Ma," said Teddy. "I'll stay here by the hole and bop him."

"I'm mending that hole right now," said Gupp.

"Mister Gupsworth, if Teddy —"

"I'm mending the hole."

Teddy glowered down on Gupp while he got the hammer, saw, and a length of wood, and went about mending the hole where Herschel was wont to come through the floor.

"Ma'd've got that rat if you hadn't pawed at her," Teddy said.

"You mind your rowing machine and I'll mind mine," said Gupp.

Mrs. Fedwick was now in the process of carrying everything outside. Chairs, utensils, bedding, tools, everything was stacked in the bright sunshine outside. Each time she carried something outside, she would scrutinize it and say — "*Humph!*" — before returning.

Gupp kept moving here and there, watching her, and keeping his eye on Teddy, too, for Teddy still was armed with the club.

"What's this?" Mrs. Fedwick asked, looking with revulsion at the flapjack can.

This ancient, thickly encrusted household essential Gupp had kept sitting winter and summer in exactly the right spot in relation to the cook stove so it would maintain the correct temperature for fermentation. The sourdough maker's art is like that of cook and wine maker's combined and Gupp had kept his starter going like Olympic fire for the past twenty years.

"Hold on," said Gupp, "that's my flapjack batter."

"It's all spoiled."

"No it ain't . . ." He was unable to stop her. She hurled it across the yard.

Gupp lurked in the house, keeping watch of his other valuables, and keeping watch of Teddy and his club. He chewed tobacco, and from time to time he carefully aimed tobacco juice through a crack where two of the floorboards failed to join.

"The floor will have to be repaired there, too," said Mrs. Fedwick.

"That's my spittin' hole."

"Well, I must say I was in hopes you wouldn't be a chewer, but, if you can't manage to break yourself of the habit, you'll have to buy one of those little china cuspidors and carry that around with you. Then, each time you use it, you can take it outside and clean it. What are those old rocks doing here?" Mrs. Fedwick now asked, indicating the ore specimens.

119

"Those are my ore specimens."

"They'll have to go out."

"I'll throw 'em out, Ma," said Teddy. "I like to throw things."

"Keep your hands offen my minerals!"

The two men faced each other and Gupp commenced gathering the specimens up, stuffing them in his pockets and loading his arms. With the most treasured of them he started for the door when the air was rent by the woman's scream.

"The rat! The rat again!"

"I'll get him, Ma!" Teddy was shouting, charging around with his club.

"Stop it!" cried Gupp, dropping the specimens. "That's not a rat, that's Herschel."

"It's a rat!" wailed Mrs. Fedwick. "There he is, Teddy. He's hiding behind the stove."

Teddy charged with his club raised and Gupp tried to get in front of him. He was no match for Teddy's size and strength, but he delayed him just long enough for the rat to scoot under the cook stove.

"He's under the stove now," Mrs. Fedwick was saying, armed with a poker. "I'll watch from this side."

Teddy bawled: "Get by the door! Don't let him get out, that's all I ask."

"That's my rat," Gupp was saying. "You ain't going to kill my rat."

Teddy shoved him away. He did not hear Gupp's shouted warnings to his mother. He got down and commenced poking beneath the stove, but the rat had gone. There was a scurry near the wood box. Teddy grabbed the box, pulled it loose from its moorings, and upended it.

The rat cowered, not knowing which way to go. The club was upraised, but Gupp grappled as it descended. His unexpected weight carried Teddy to the wall.

"You made me miss the rat, you danged old fool!" Teddy shouted.

"You leave my rat alone!" Gupp backed up, looking for a weapon, but his picks and shovels and old Martha, his shotgun, were all outside. "I may not be so young, and I may not have muscles from a correspondence school, but just the same nobody's going to come in my cabin and throw out my pancake batter and my ore specimens and then kill my rat . . . you and your chiny spittoons, your exercisers, and your rowing machine . . ."

"This is the house where Ma and I are going to live and we're not going to put up with any rat."

"There he is!" screamed Mrs. Fedwick.

Gupp wrestled for the club. The rat scurried past them heading for the hole in the floor but, alas, Gupp had mended it. He tarried for an instant, only an instant, but the momentary pause had sealed his fate. The poker in the hands of Mrs. Fedwick descended, and the rat lay still.

"There!" said Mrs. Fedwick, blowing her breath. "I guess that settles that."

For an instant Gupp stared down at the dead rat. He walked to the door.

"Pick up the awful thing," Mrs. Fedwick was saying. "I can't bear to touch it."

121

Gupp went outside. There was his old ten-gauge double. He took a look to see that it was loaded. He advanced to the door, bent over the gun with both its hammers cocked.

"You varmints," he said, "git to packing!"

"You old fool," said Mrs. Fedwick, "put down that gun."

"Git out of my house, the both of you, and git out quick, or you'll be picking birdshot out o' your hide clean from here to Champa Street."

Mrs. Fedwick tried to parry. "Why, Mister Gupsworth, this is a peculiar attitude for you to take. Put up that gun . . ."

"Don't you try anything," Gupp said, attempting to watch both of them at the same time.

"All right," said Teddy, "let us get our stuff out."

Gupp lowered the gun. He just knew what Teddy would try and was ready for him. As Teddy swung a haymaker at his head, he bent double, brought the gun up butt first, driving it deeply into Teddy's belly.

"*Oof!*" said Teddy, his jaw limp and his knees sagging.

"So you did, did you?" said Gupp. "So you took lessons from Lionel Strongfort! Well, let me tell you about another Teddy I knew one time and a thing I learned offen him. Teddy Roosevelt and the old Rough Riders, and here's my Cuban special!"

Gupp swung up with his fist but he let his arm double over at the last instant, bringing instead his bent elbow into crashing contact with Teddy's jaw.

122

Teddy staggered to the wall, and, when he rebounded, Gupp whooped: "And this I named my single-jack punch, developed right up yonder in the U.S. Mint!"

Mrs. Fedwick clawed a handful of Gupp's hair, pulling him away.

"Git away from me, you pink-plumed catymount!"

He lifted the side of one freshly tallowed boot, catching her fairly in the place where he had aimed. Then, with the gun once more aimed, he said: "Git your stuff and git to packin', and, if I see you inside of the lines of the U.S. Mint patent survey once after sundown, I'll show you how I deal with claim-jumpers."

It seemed unusually quiet when they were gone. He buried the rat and carried everything back inside, putting it exactly as it had been before Mrs. Fedwick and her boy arrived.

He imagined they got a ride back on the mud wagon. He did not check to see. The minister did not arrive, so he supposed they had seen him and turned him back. It suited Gupp just as well. He wanted nothing to remind him of them.

He rescued his sourdough can and found a heel of the starter and added warm water and flour to it. He cooked baking-powder biscuits and salt pork for supper, using the can that sat in its correct spot between the lead carbonate and the cyanide. He even caught himself whistling "Buffalo Gals", and stopped with a pang.

He slept and arose next morning, and worked all day in the U.S. Mint. He worked extra long each day, trying to leave home earlier than usual and come home later so as to forget about Herschel.

One morning, with a cold drizzle of rain outside, he found himself whistling "Buffalo Gals" while frying pancakes on the cook stove. He stopped, hearing a rustle of movement beneath the floor. It was almost like Herschel had come back.

He got the hammer and pulled the mended portion of floor away, and into the room came a pack rat. It *was* Herschel. There could be no doubt about it. It was Herschel!

In amazement he watched as other forms followed, little rats, almost transparent they looked, with bits of jet in their eyes and the tips of their noses, baby pack rats, five of them.

"Well," Gupp said, "you can blast me on a short fuse!"

He understood then. The other pack rat, the dead one, had come from town in that carton of groceries. That rat had escaped beneath the floor and become Herschel's wife.

No, come to think of it, that rat was Herschel's husband!

Outcasts of the Storm

CHAPTER ONE

It was no more than twenty miles from the railhead at Prince Albert to Vermilion Landing at the northern end of Chilkoos Lake, but the paddle-wheel steamboat puffed and splashed through most of the autumn day in making it. At last the captain expended a quantity of its precious steam in one long blast of the whistle and came down the steps from the hurricane deck, buttoning his blue officer's coat.

"Vermilion," he said to the boat's one passenger.

As a rule, even on Tuesdays the boat could count on at least half a dozen passengers, generally timber jacks, returning to the camps beyond Vermilion, broke and battered after a spree in the saloons of Prince Albert, but this time there was only this tall, broad-shouldered young man from "outside". He wore a red and black Mackinaw, stagged wool trousers, and calked boots, but they still had a brand-new look about them, and there were other less obvious things that set him apart from the ordinary run of timber stiffs and accounted for the captain's deference when he went on: "I doubt there'll be a train up the narrow gauge before tomorrow morning, but I dare say Burgess can find room for you in the Company bunkhouse. You'd need blankets, though."

"I'll get by."

The young man wasn't handsome, but he had a smile the captain liked, and after thinking a moment he said: "If you'd like, you can sleep here on the boat. We don't go back till sunup."

"Thanks, but I'm in a hurry to get into the back country."

"For Talka?"

"No, for Chipman."

The captain stopped abruptly and looked at him. "Oh, to Chipman."

Three years had passed since Tim Chipman had visited the timber camp founded by his father and uncle, but according to his recollection it was the most logical destination of anyone using the steamboat landing at Vermilion. Apparently things had changed. The captain suddenly lost all desire to talk and walked down the deck, shouting orders to a crewman about getting the shore line in readiness, an unnecessary command because the crewman already had the coiled hawser in his hands.

Tim Chipman watched him as a troubled furrow appeared above the bridge of his nose. Things had changed since he'd gone away to college three years before. He'd sensed it during his short stop in Prince Albert that morning, just as he'd sensed it four days ago when he received the telegram from Steve Riika, his uncle's timber boss. The message read:

You come back now. You come back quick now, Tim. You hurry up and see Clay.

And so he'd packed his things and come. Three years. He stood by the rail, watching the docks of Vermilion Landing take form through the purplish, autumn mist that lay over the north woods lake. A new overhead crane had been installed, and there were some long, red-painted sheds that hadn't been there before. It was a while before the lettering on their roofs became discernible: **Talka River Timber Company.** As a boy he remembered the Talka River outfit as a small concern operating custom mills near Vermilion and down the West Arm, at Sista Landing. Business had gone ahead with Talka since Croft Brunner took over. It gave Tim an uneasy feeling. During his first year away in the States, his uncle, Clay Chipman, had written a great deal about the business, but for the last year his letters had contained nothing definite, merely the general assurance that things were all right and that he wanted Tim to stay on at college and finish his engineering studies in the shortest possible time rather than waste a summer by coming home.

The boat rubbed its side along the dock pilings and Tim Chipman hoisted his suitcase and plunder bag to his shoulder, carrying them ashore timber-jack style. New planking had been laid on the dock. A barge was loaded to its waterline with bolts of new-cut cedar. He noticed that the butt end of each bolt carried the T and Circle brand of the Talka River Company. No Chipman logs or bolts. The old Chipman loading crane had a rusty, disused look. He walked on across the docks and up a corduroy walk to the Vermilion trading post.

The trading post, at least, looked the same as ever. Its windows apparently had not been washed since he left. The same moose antlers were nailed over the door, the same Beaver Indians sat on the bench outside, eating candy bars. He spoke to them, pausing in the door to let his eyes become accustomed to the dim interior. Cade Burgess, a heavy, middle-aged man, was standing behind the counter, looking at him.

"Hello, Cade," Tim said.

It was a moment before Burgess recognized him. Then his eyes narrowed and he drew his lips away from his tobacco-browned teeth in what was intended as a smile. "Why, Tim, I thought you'd gone to the States for good." They shook hands, and Burgess asked: "Come on account of Clay?"

"Yes. What about Clay?"

"Why, I thought you'd know." He stalled for time by adjusting his sleeve protectors. "He's . . . hard up. He got hurt, you know."

"No, I didn't. How badly is he hurt?"

"I . . . don't know. Ain't been anybody down for . . ."

"What happened?"

"I hear there was a fight. Nobody knows. They just found him there, beat up. They took him back to camp, but I guess he ain't come to."

"Where'd they find him?"

"On the road back from his north camp, I hear. Damn it, I haven't been up there."

Burgess knew more than he was willing to say.

"What's wrong around here anyway?"

"I don't know anything about it. I keep my nose out of —"

Tim Chipman moved quickly. His arm reached across the counter; he seized Burgess by the front of his rough, gray shirt and dragged him forward. Burgess was thirty or forty pounds lighter than Tim but he was strong, and the struggle he put up threatened to tip the counter over. Tim dragged him farther and farther forward. At last Burgess stopped fighting and was satisfied to get what breath he could through his constricted shirt collar.

"I asked what was going on here!"

"Take your ha —"

"There's a fight going on between Chipman and the Talka Company, isn't there?"

"Clay was having trouble with Brunner. Listen, Tim, I just run this store for him. He don't tell me nothing. I just shovel up his beans and collect money."

Tim let go, and Burgess staggered back. He used the shelves for support while getting his wind. "You Chipmans always was a strong-arm bunch. That's why you . . . Look what you done to my shirt."

"You're working for Brunner?" The store had been owned by the Swiftwater Company when Tim had left. "Brunner seems to have taken over."

"I told you. I didn't . . ."

"All right, you don't know."

Tim didn't want to slap it out of him. He'd find out that night.

Brunner. He remembered the man well enough. He should. Croft Brunner had been boss of that Rouge River log drive eight years before when 5,000,000 board feet of Chipman saw logs disappeared on Chilkoos Lake. Tim's father Pat had called him a thief that night when they were drying off at a campfire by the mouth of the Rouge, and Brunner had responded by smashing him across the mouth. He'd have gone on that night and given Pat the hobs even though Pat was past fifty with a cough settled in his lungs that later cost him his life, but the others jumped in and stopped it. After that, Brunner had been successively a log pirate, a wildcat logging operator, and finally the owner of this old Talka River outfit.

Tim said: "There's no train tonight, I suppose?"

A crank-up telephone was fixed to the wall back of the counter but Burgess made no suggestion that Tim use it.

"I'd like to phone for a speeder."

"Phone to Chipman? Why, there ain't been a phone wire working up there for six, eight months."

"Why?"

"I don't concern myself . . ."

"Yes, I know. You just shovel up beans and don't ask about things that don't concern you." Tim Chipman laughed, and hoisted the suitcase and plunder bag to one shoulder. "How's the walking? Or haven't they got ground running up that far?"

He went outside, stood for a while beneath the pale awning. He glanced back inside before starting toward

132

the railroad. Burgess was furiously operating the crank of the telephone.

No one was around the depot of the little narrow-gauge railway that the Chipman, Talka, and Swiftwater companies had built as a co-operative venture twelve years before. He opened the door to a tool house. A couple of handcars stood inside. One of them he remembered operating as a boy. He lifted it out, smeared some grease on the gears, and started up the grade from town, driving it swiftly with easy, one-handed strokes.

The sun was still up, but it had turned reddish from autumn mists that hung near the horizon and there was no heat in it. A wind blew from the north, carrying forest odors and a feel of snowfields. Winter was not far away. Already he could see edgings of white along the higher hilltops. The grade steepened, and he had a chance to stretch his muscles — muscles that he hadn't called into use even while winning his reputation as the best tackle Western Tech had ever had.

The road skirted a steep-sided gulch for about three miles, then it wandered in long curves following hill contours. The land had been cut over, but long before, and in another ten years the pulp buyers would be bidding for the second-growth spruce that covered it. It was late evening when he pumped the handcar around a bend and saw the Talka Camp, lying beneath a blue layer of smoke from its mills. Things had obviously picked up under Brunner's direction. The camp seemed to have doubled in size, there was a new wing on the mill, and a vast expansion of the drying yards.

The switch had been left open by the train crew when they took the wagons and a string of flatcars down to the yard platform. He stopped, lifted the handcar over the switch, and went on, leaving Talka behind.

The valley narrowed and there was a steepening of the railroad grade. Fatigue and deep breathing in the open air slowly glazed his mind, and it was like awakening from a half sleep when someone shouted. His senses were instantly acute, and he saw three men in the tracks ahead of him. Beyond them, a cribwork of timbers had been erected to block the track.

He let up on the handles, and the handcar slowed quickly against the grade. Two of the men remained where they were, near the barricade, while the third, a massive Swede, plodded down the track, swinging an axe handle in his hand. He stopped and planted his feet widely, evidently intending to block the handcar with his body, but it came to a stop a couple of feet away. There was an expression of truculent stubbornness on his face. His small, pale eyes shifted from the handcar and came to rest on Tim's face.

"Whar you tank you goin'?"

His voice was a rumble from the depths of a massive chest. He kept swinging the axe handle back and forth, pendulum fashion. He was no taller than Chipman, but broader and thicker in the limbs, so he exceeded him by sixty or seventy pounds in weight. As is the case with many men of tremendous bulk, it was impossible to guess his age.

134

Chipman stepped off the handcar and took time to block the wheels.

"Whar you goin'?" the Swede roared, apparently enraged that his question hadn't been answered.

"Think it's any of your business?" Chipman walked around the handcar and looked in the man's pale eyes. It seemed to take a while for the words to register, and before another roar of rage could come from the Swede's throat, he went on: "Get that barricade out of the way."

One of the other men stirred himself from the barricade and laughed. "The brave bucko! Now did you hear that, Ole? This young sport's got it on his mind to go to Chipman!"

Ole stood for a while, letting the idea sink through his mind. Then he decided to laugh, too. "Yah. So you bane goin' up to Chipman on handcar. By golly, that's good yoke."

Ole stopped laughing and his face became more truculent and stubborn than ever. He lifted the axe handle overhead as though it were some sort of standard and said: "You know who you bane talkin' to? You know Aye bane Axe-Handle Ole?"

"Never heard of you."

"Hah? You don't ever har of Axe-Handle Ole? By Yimminy, you lie to me, Aye got big good notion to break your neck with this geude hickory axe handle."

"Sing him your song, Ole," one of the men said.

"By golly, yah. Aye skol sing song. Then he bane har about Axe-Handle Ole all right." He thereupon peeled

135

back his lips and started to bellow a variation of the old timber-jack's song.

> My name is bane Yonson
> Aye come from Wisconsin
> Aye work in the hardwood stand,
> Aye come to Shee-baggin
> On Yim Hill's red wagon
> Wit' axe handle in my hand.

Ole must have had a quart cached somewhere in the nearby bush for, as he sang, Chipman could smell the whiskey on his breath. He finished the verse, took a huge breath, and stamped his heavy, hobnailed boots while roaring forth the chorus.

> Aye wear a red collar
> Aye drank sixteen dollar
> Wit' axe handle in my hand.

Singing the song made Axe-Handle Ole feel good all over. For the moment he'd forgotten all about Chipman's existence. Then his eyes fell on him again.

"You still har? Didn't you har Axe-Handle Ole say you better go back down tracks?"

Ole drew himself back in a manner designed to make Chipman quail before his tremendous size. The axe handle was flourished high. He started forward, evidently expecting him to retreat. Instead, Tim Chipman shifted his feet, took half a step forward, and smashed a left and right to his jaw.

Ole took the blows. They jolted his head and he was on his heels for an instant, but he did not go down. He merely seemed to absorb the force of them. The axe handle was still high. He grunted and swung it down with a force that would have split Tim Chipman's skull, but he'd been ready and moved aside.

Missing the blow carried Axe-Handle Ole off balance. He was turned partly away, his jaw unprotected, and Tim hit him again. It was perfectly timed, combining the snap and strength of his back and shoulder, but Ole was still on his feet. He had a brute brain that absorbed punishment and became heavy from it like a sponge takes water, but little short of a sledge would put him down and out.

He started to turn, tripped, lost his balance. He was in a sitting position with the axe handle beside him. His eyes roved; it took them a while to get focused on his assailant. Then he realized that he, the mighty Axe-Handle Ole, was down, with this raw-boned young man standing over him. He twisted over on hands and feet, crouched like a sprinter.

"So. You goin' fight Axe-Handle Ole. By golly, that's geude. Ole rather fight than eat lutefisk and drink whiskey, by golly."

He tossed the axe handle aside and charged. Big as Tim Chipman was, he knew better than try to meet the man head on. He side-stepped at the last instant, thinking Ole would go past him. The big Swede was quicker than any man would expect. He turned and forced Chipman back. Retreating, Tim swung another left and right. There was no trick to hitting the big man,

137

but it seemed futile, for he merely took the blows and kept coming.

The railroad grade slanted steeply behind Chipman's heels. He tried to get his balance. The huge man was atop him. They rolled and crashed deep in buck brush. Ole let his momentum carry him on, came to his feet, dragging Chipman by the Mackinaw. Ole swung his fist in a short arc. He bent his arm at the final instant. The fist deliberately missed its mark and his elbow struck with the stunning impact of a club.

Force of the blow smashed Tim backward with the buttons tearing off his Mackinaw. He fell, landing on his back. Instinctively he doubled both legs, with knees beneath his chin. Ole was charging in. He tried to stop at the last instant. It was too late. Tim's legs uncoiled and his hobnailed boots took Ole in the stomach. Ole grunted, backpedaled, went down.

It was Tim's chance. He'd been raised in the deep timber and had watched a hundred brutal loggers' fights. He knew the rules, or lack of them. So now that he had the man down, he did not hesitate. He rolled to his feet, ready to charge and drive his hobs to the side of Ole's head.

Someone was behind him. He started to turn, but there was no time. A blow sent him staggering off balance. One of the other men had clubbed him in the back of the neck with a fist weighted by a railroad spike. Tim mounted to stay on his feet, but the blow had given Ole his chance.

The huge man was up, coming for him. Tim tried to move and swing his fists, but the blow had slowed him.

He was like one moving in a nightmare. He knew Ole was swinging a fist to his jaw, but he was unable to do anything about it.

He was down, with rough stones of the railroad grade under his hands. He knew that Ole was lifting him, knew when he was smashed down again. It happened a couple of times before a blackness darker than night covered him.

CHAPTER
TWO

Regaining consciousness was a tortuous process, a time of fighting his way up through successive layers of nightmare and pain until at last he knew that his eyes were open and that light was hurting them. He closed his eyes tightly. Pain kept knifing down through the middle of his skull and the back of his neck. He lay still and scarcely breathed. That way the pain became less, and finally vanished altogether. It seemed that he'd remained in that position for an hour or more, although probably the time was much shorter. Finally little things began to be noticeable. A fire snapped somewhere, and the air held an odor of burning pine. There was a slight creak of flooring as someone moved nearby. He opened his eyes. A girl was looking down on him, a blonde girl, unexpectedly beautiful. She was not exactly a stranger. He remained as he was, looking up into her face. He knew he'd seen her somewhere.

"How do you feel?" she asked.

"Better." His lips and the left side of his face felt stiff. Ole had trampled him beneath his hobs. He licked his lips and went on, "Don't move. Just stand there."

140

She did as he asked. A light was burning behind her, forming an aura of brightness around her blonde hair, making it seem as fine as silk floss.

"Can I move now?" she said.

"I was trying to remember where I'd seen you before."

"I'm Lynne Tilton."

He remembered her then. Lynne Tilton, daughter of old Swiftwater Tilton, owner of the Swiftwater Lumber Company. The Tiltons had lived in one of the big houses atop the hill in Prince Albert, and, although his own family had timber holdings as far-flung as hers, he'd always felt uncomfortable in her presence. She'd been small, and exquisite in a way that made him feel like a big-footed country boy. But that had been a long time ago. She'd changed now, and he'd changed, too.

"You remember me?" he asked.

"Yes. You're Tim Chipman. I'd been expecting you'd come."

He sat up. Pain seemed to split his skull down the middle and things blanked out for a moment. He remained sitting in the pine bunk, holding its sides until he'd steadied himself. Then he turned and got his feet on the floor.

"I guess someone else was expecting me."

"I'm sorry."

"Axe-Handle Ole isn't one of your Swiftwater men?"

"He was there doing a job. I guess he tried to do it too well."

"What do you mean . . . doing a job?"

141

"The railroad's no longer open to the Chipman Camp."

"Why?"

She hunted for an explanation, and, when no ready words came, a flush mounted to her cheeks. "It's a long story. Maybe you don't realize the things that have been going on here since you left."

"I don't believe I do."

"There's been trouble about the railroad. I don't understand all the angles of it, but it boils down to the fact that the road was falling apart and your uncle refused to pay his share in fixing it up. Swiftwater and the Talka River Company owned two-thirds of it, so they went ahead with the job."

"And closed the line beyond your north boundary."

"Yes."

"Ole's doing a good job of it. Tell your dad and Brunner to raise his pay."

"I'm sorry it happened, Tim. Ole shouldn't have gone that far. I sent word to Croft about it."

"Croft." He was thinking it was a last name, then he remembered — it would be Croft Brunner, owner of the Talka Company.

"Croft Brunner?"

"Why, yes. Croft Brunner."

There was a certain way in which she said his name. He shot a glance at her and a flush appeared in her cheeks.

To change the subject, she said: "I was sorry about your uncle."

142

The tone of her words came as a jolt to him. "What about my uncle?"

"You didn't hear about Clay? He's . . . dead. He died three days ago. They found him outside the camp and he never regained consciousness. There'd been a fight. His skull was fractured."

Tim Chipman stood up, looming tall and broad-shouldered, his head almost touching a low beam of the ceiling. The expression on his face made her fall back half a step.

"Tim! Don't get the idea . . ."

"Don't get what idea? That Axe-Handle Ole went up there after him? I don't know anything about it. Except by the way Burgess acted."

"What about Burgess?"

"Nothing."

"If Burgess said we had anything to do with it, he wasn't telling the truth. Clay had had trouble with his men. He hadn't been paying them more than half their wages for the last five or six months. If you want to find the ones who did it, the place for you to go is up there to Chipman."

"All right. I don't know anything about it, but I'll find out." His scalp felt dry and itchy from the beating he'd taken. He ran fingers through his hair. It was stiff along one side from dried blood. "Funny how us Chipmans seem to get it in the skull."

Draft started the lamp flame fluttering. A door had opened somewhere. There were sounds of its closing, then the thud of a man's boots as he walked along the short length of hallway leading to the room. He paused just outside, only his shadowy outline visible in the long rays of the lamp. He was a big man, shorter but broader than Tim Chipman. They probably weighed about the same.

His eyes were on Tim and the girl, but he took time to remove his Mackinaw and hat and hang them on a set of deer antlers that served as a coat rack.

Then he spoke: "You weren't flattened out there tonight because you were a Chipman."

The man was Croft Brunner. His voice was unforgettable. It was a strong voice, one that would have been envied by a public speaker, although perhaps there was a little too much command in his inflection. He walked on inside the room. He looked as though he'd gained fifteen or twenty pounds since that night down by the mouth of the Rouge, but none of it was fat. He was handsome in a heavy-jawed way, about thirty-four. Years before, someone had struck him with a peavey, splitting the skin near his right eye so it healed with a puckery scar, and it gave that side of his face a squinty look. He wore rough wool, and there was mud and sawdust ground into it like the clothes of any timber stiff, but no one would have mistaken him for one. There was something in his manner that stamped him as the big *tyee*.

He went on talking. "No, you being a Chipman had nothing to do with it. I'm sorry it happened. Sorry about Clay, too. We had our differences, but I always liked him." He stretched out his hand. "Glad to see you, Tim. I hope you can straighten things out up there."

144

Tim Chipman was still grim-faced from the shock of hearing about his uncle. He shook Brunner's hand. The man was trying to seem sincere, and he was a good actor, but Tim knew how he hated everyone by the name of Chipman since that day on the Rouge.

"You started by straightening *me* out, anyway," he said.

Brunner dropped his hand and stepped back. His eyes were narrow, intent on Tim's face. "Don't make an issue of it, Tim. I'm sorry for Ole putting the cooler on you out there, but it wouldn't have happened if you hadn't practically dared him into it."

Anger was flowing through Tim Chipman's frame, but he was controlling the outward signs of it well enough. His voice was a trifle softer than usual, and there was an easy contempt in his manner. "It just happens that my father built that logging road, and no big-footed Swede with an axe handle in his hand is going to stop me from going through."

"You're here," Brunner said.

"But I'm still going through."

"I said not to make an issue of it!"

"That sounded like an order."

Lynne Tilton had watched the two men as their tempers mounted. She took a step forward and touched Brunner on the arm. He moved suddenly as though her hand surprised him. "Oh, Lynne!"

"Croft, don't let's have any trouble. Not here . . . tonight."

Tim Chipman saw a race of white reflection across the third finger of her left hand, and he knew by that,

145

together with her manner toward Croft Brunner, that she was engaged to marry him. It shouldn't have made any difference. He'd almost forgotten about the girl's existence until a few minutes ago, but the thought of her marrying Brunner made the room seem too warm for him.

Brunner smiled down at her. There was an unexpected gentleness in his manner. He really cared for the girl. It was something of a shock to know that Brunner could feel like that toward anyone.

"Yes, Lynne." He turned to Tim and said: "She's right. If we have to get rough, this is no place for it." He walked to the massive, hand-hewn mantel, lifted down a bottle of H.B.C. Scotch and two glasses, put them down on a table. "I think a drink would do us both some good."

Anger made Tim's hand tremble a little, but he poured the tiny glass full without getting any on the table. He waited for Brunner who took only a few drops. They drank together.

"You've been gone a long time, Tim."

"Three years."

"School? Engineering, I understand."

"Yes."

"I went to school one time. I got through my seventh reader. From there, I was on my own. I went to work in a timber camp. I was flunky for the crumb boss. That was over at MacCloud. The big *tyee* was a Britisher by the name of Stenlee. He'd graduated from a German university, and, when he came there, he didn't know the difference between bull pine and Stika spruce. But

146

he knew some other things. He could stand there with his slide rule and figure more timber in five minutes than our boss logger could cipher out with pencil and paper all winter. The timber stiffs laughed at him behind his back, but all the same he was the one living in the big house. I made up my mind right then I'd never be just a strong-armed stiff in a pair of tin pants. I used to go up there and flunky around the kitchen. Every once in a while I'd swipe one of his books and after everybody was in their bunks read it. Then I'd take it back and swipe another. Sometimes I used to fall asleep on my feet next day and the crumb boss would take it out of my hide with a skillet. Nobody ever gave it to me on a Wedgewood dish. But I got it."

Tim wondered if he was talking for the girl's benefit, and decided that he wasn't. He was talking more for himself than anyone, proving to himself that he was better than any Chipman.

He restoppered the whiskey and went on: "I got it the hard way, Tim, so maybe that's why I value things more than most men. Look at this Talka concern. It was held together by haywire and mortgages, but I picked it up and made it pay. I'm going to keep on making it pay, and nobody is going to ride on my shoulders. Clay's dead, and I don't want to say anything against him. Now you're here. You'll be taking over, I suppose. Or do you plan to save what you can and get out?"

"I'll stay."

Brunner met his eyes. He was smiling a very little. "You sound sure of that."

"I'll stay," Tim repeated.

"You'll have a hard time operating up there without the railroad to Vermilion. I don't want to be rough on you. You'll get the same break on it that we do as soon as you pay your share for repairing it."

"How much is that?"

"Offhand . . . eleven thousand. You'll find enough statements for the amount when you get up there. Unless Clay threw them away."

"That was your whole trouble with Clay?"

"No." He paced the room and stood with his powerful legs set widely, hands clasped behind his back, warming them at the fire. "You wouldn't have known your uncle the last couple of years, Tim. He got sort of . . . queer. Thought everybody was trying to get him from behind. You know how Chipman, Talka, and the Swiftwater have always worked. We've never paid attention to boundary lines. If we needed to cross another's territory to yard some logs, we did it. I needed to use three miles of railroad on his cut-over Treaty lands to log that North Boundary tract. He stopped me with a gang of men who weren't loggers. They were toughs he hired out of those Prince Albert saloons."

"Fellows like Axe-Handle Ole."

The thrust angered him. "I was trying to be decent about this, Chipman!"

Tim laughed without sounding good-humored. He looked around for his hat. Lynne handed it to him. She didn't say anything, but there was a pleading expression in her eyes. She was asking him to understand Croft Brunner's position. He thanked her, and walked toward the door. Brunner didn't offer to go with him. He still stood by the fire, warming his hands behind him. "My handcar still up there?" Tim asked.

"The handcar has been taken down to the shed. You're not taking railroad property through that barricade. The road will stay blocked until every dime of your share is paid. I never rode on Chipman shoulders, and they're not going to ride on mine."

"I always had an idea we'd started you in the timber business."

He was calling Brunner a thief, just about as plainly as Pat Chipman had called him one that night at the mouth of the Rouge. The words struck Brunner and he started almost as though he intended to charge across the room. He checked himself. His muscles had made the shoulders of his flannel shirt grow tight. His face darkened beneath his windburn. It had a lean, savage look. He spoke: "You chose your spot to say that, Chipman. Here, in this house, where you're Lynne's guest. Don't ever try saying it to me again."

"I was slugged and carried here, if you call that being a guest." He looked at the girl. "I'm sorry, Lynne. I'll be going now."

His suitcase and bundle were standing in the hall. He took them and went outside. It had been dark for more than an hour, and the night wind had carried some of the smoke away, revealing the moon. He'd been inside the headquarters house, a long, log- and rough-lumber building with a porch on two sides of it. There was a company store nearby, and beyond that some rows of one-room shacks where the mill crew lived. Men were sitting along the store's platform sidewalk, watching him.

They'd been talking, but they stopped on seeing who he was. He walked down the three steps from the porch, followed a corduroy sidewalk, and would have gone past without saying anything, but someone moved and stood. A huge fellow. Familiar. It was Axe-Handle Ole.

Tim put out his hand.

"Ole, you're a strong fellow," he said.

Ole was guarded and suspicious. "Yah."

"You're a great fighting man, Ole. I always liked a good fighting man. The Chipmans have always been good fighting men, too. Did you know that, Ole?"

"Yah."

"You fooled me up there by the tricks, Ole. You were too quick for me. I didn't think you were such a smart fighting man, Ole."

"Hah!" Axe-Handle Ole had expected trouble, but these things were good to hear. He chuckled and snapped his suspenders. "Yah, Aye been in lots of geude fights. By golly, Aye been in too many fights to get fooled much."

"There's just one thing . . ."

The suspicion returned. "Yah?"

"You don't know how to use that axe handle. Somebody's going to take it away from you sometime and beat you over the head with it."

The grin was gone from Ole's vast face. He reared himself to full height and swelled his chest. It was a posture he'd learned by practicing in front of saloon

150

mirrors before wrecking the joints, and he assumed it now to awe Chipman into the ground before him. "Ho! You tank maybe you could take axe handle away? You maybe . . ."

"Sure. I'll take it away from you."

"By golly, you har what he say? He tank he can take axe handle away from Ole! Ain't two men . . . ain't three men in whole big nort' woods strong enough to take axe handle away from Ole. You har me say that?"

"Yes, I heard you."

Somebody spoke from the shadowy porch: "Go ahead, Ole. Let's see him do it."

Ole hesitated. "Boss, he say Aye shouldn't make trouble, so . . ."

It was Chipman's turn to laugh, and he did a good, contemptuous job of it.

"So! You tank Ole scared? You coom up har. Har's axe handle, by golly. Now you try to take it away, yah." Ole stood with his feet planted widely, his shoulders thrown back, the axe handle in his right hand, thrust far out. "You go ahead. Aye let you use two hands, and Ole yust use one."

Tim grabbed the axe handle just below Ole's hand. He jerked back, but the handle was solid as though anchored at the end of a six-inch beam. Little by little, a smile spread across Ole's face.

"Don't pull so hard, noo. You skol twist Ole's arm out at socket, by Yimminy."

Tim rammed forward. The movement was unexpected and it made Ole stagger half a step. An instant later, Tim seized the axe handle with both hands and sprang

151

onto his back, setting his boots against Ole's groin. Ole tried to stay on his feet, but Tim's weight was enough to unbalance him. He fell face forward. Tim twisted over and jammed the axe handle against the plank platform. It was like a vaulting pole, carrying Ole forward. His hands lost their grip on the handle as he sailed on and scrubbed face down across the walk.

Ole got to hands and knees. One side of his face was full of splinters. He was slightly stunned. He shook his head back and forth, looking like a beef that had dragged itself up after being struck by a mallet. His eyes focused on Tim, and he charged.

Tim had the axe handle now and swung it to smash him aside, but Ole caught most of the force with an upflung forearm. His charge carried Tim half the length of the sidewalk. He let the axe handle fall and smashed rights and lefts to the big Swede's head. Ole tried to return them. He had a massive strength, but he'd never learned the boxer's art of bringing his punches to an apex. One of his blows swept Tim aside and left him between the fuel box and the building's log front.

A door had opened and closed and someone was running that way.

"Ole!" Brunner shouted.

Ole did not hesitate. He charged on, trying to corner his man. Instead of using his fists this time, he sprang, boots first, but Tim slid aside and Ole's hobs tore slivers from the store front.

"Stop it!" Brunner cried.

152

"No, Aye won't stop. Aye skol give him what that other Chipman got, by golly. Skol give him what old Clay Chipman . . ."

Brunner covered the distance with a series of leaping strides. He grabbed Ole and spun him around. Ole had his hands part way up, looking at Brunner with half-comprehending eyes. He saw the blow start, but there was no time to fend it off. Brunner's left fist put Ole back on his heels. The right came with the impact of a sledge, smashing him off the platform.

Ole spun and went down on his face. He lay for five or six seconds without moving. Then slowly he got his knees under him, groped for the platform with one hand, looked up, blinking dirt and fragments of spruce needles from his eyelashes.

Brunner stood on the platform, looking down at him with undisguised contempt. He kept opening and closing his right hand. The knuckles were skinned and oozing blood. He sucked at them, shook out a handkerchief, wrapped it like a bandage.

"That's a good right hand you have, Brunner," Tim Chipman said.

Brunner turned and watched Chipman's eyes, wondering how much he'd guessed from Ole's words.

"Say what's on your mind!"

"I did. That's a good right hand."

Tim Chipman hoisted his things back on one shoulder and walked off through the early afternoon.

CHAPTER
THREE

Two men watched from the barricade, silent and suspicious, but they made no move to stop him. Tim spoke, and one of them grunted an answer. A Winchester rifle was leaning in the shadow of the barricade, making a dull, blue reflection. They were ready for anything.

The moon faded behind successive veils of fog as he walked through forest up the disused railway. It was getting colder, and little pellets of snow started to crystallize from the atmosphere and settle in low places along the track. After an hour, each tie was outlined in white that glowed like phosphorescence in the dark.

It was midnight when he reached the camp of Chipman. He stopped for a while to look at it. He'd remembered it as being larger. Time had changed his perspective. Darkness and snow made it look drab and abandoned. Lights burned in a couple of bunkhouse windows. That was where the woods boss, Steve Riika, had his office. There were more bunkhouses, the cook house, cache house, wagon shack, and company office, forming sort of a street. Down a slight hill, overlooking the Talka River, he could see the broad roofs of the bolt mill and drying sheds, shining dimly from their thin covering of snow.

As he watched, a billow of sparks rose from the bunkhouse chimney, so he knew that someone had just added wood to the fire. He started down, following a shortcut path. After forty or fifty steps, the night silence was cut by the sharp *click* of a gun hammer being drawn to cock.

The sound had come from the shadow of a massive cedar tree. He stopped, careful to make no movement that might be misinterpreted, and slowly turned. He could see a man coming toward him with a rifle over his arm.

"I'm Tim Chipman," he said.

"Clay's nephew?"

"Yes."

Tim had never seen the man before, but there was nothing about him that suggested he was one of the saloon toughs that Brunner had accused Clay of hiring.

"You got a match?" the man asked.

"Yes."

"Light it."

Tim scratched the match. The flame cast a ruddy light on his face.

"I guess you're a Chipman right enough. Steve's been expecting you."

Tim pointed to the gun. "Is that thing really necessary?"

"I guess so. Steve's scared they'd try something before you got here."

Tim walked on and opened the door to the bunkhouse. Steve Riika had been hunched over a big, rough-board table, his work-gnarled fingers bent around a stub pencil, writing with tortured slowness in a ledger. He looked around and got up suddenly when he saw who it was.

"Tim! I'm afraid you don't get my message. I'm afraid . . ."

"He's dead?"

"Clay? Yah. They kill him."

"Who?"

"I tell you. You sit down, I tell you. I know you Chipmans get awful mad and do crazy things. So you sit down and don't do nothing till after you sleep . . ."

"Was it Brunner?"

"They been fightin' for one, two year. Sometimes I think I set down and write you letter, but I don't. Now I wish I had."

Steve was about fifty-five with intense blue eyes and gray hair that made a marked contrast to his deeply tanned skin. Like many Finlanders, he had small, almost delicate features that seemed ill-suited to his obvious strength.

Tim went over and sat down. "Tell me about it. About Clay."

"Yah. Well, they been fightin' year and half now. Brunner and Clay. I know pretty soon somebody get killed. Brunner close the railroad, Clay fight his loggers off the North Boundary tract. Then two weeks ago Brunner come down here and tried to buy your uncle

156

out. He's got guts, that Brunner. All alone he walk down here from that speeder . . ."

"How about Clay?" Tim asked with weary insistence.

"Sure, now, I come to that," Steve said, but instead he went ahead with an account of how Brunner had attempted a road to his North Boundary tract and how Clay with five men had blasted a hillside over it. That had been a month before, and they'd been expecting retaliation ever since. Then Clay went to Nokewin Lake to look at some Douglas spruce he was logging. They'd expected him all day Thursday. On Friday, one of the teamsters found him three miles out the west road. He'd been given a brutal beating. They carried him in but he didn't regain consciousness. "We get doc down from Beaver Lake. No good. One day, two day, three day. Pretty soon . . ." Steve snapped his fingers. "We bury him yesterday, Tim."

They talked until dawn, and Tim spent next day going through the company books. No pay days had been missed. Clay had been eking out his expenses by logging some Douglas fir on the steep slopes of Nokewin Lake, from where it could be rafted twenty miles to the mills of Silver Junction on a branch line of the C.N.R. Supplies came by means of *bateau* up Nokewin, and over the Granite Knob ridge to the north in wagons. Nokewin, however, would soon be frozen, and Brunner would be in a position to sit tight and starve them out.

Tim threw the books in a corner, made up a wolf pack for himself, and set off on foot, reaching the camp at Nokewin after spending a night in the woods. From there he cruised the remaining Chipman holdings. He saw some vast areas of saw timber, only a small percentage of which could be logged in any foreseeable future, and none, aside from the Nokewin Lake fir, that could reach market without using the railroad.

He'd been back at headquarters camp only long enough to eat breakfast when a load of men came into sight, riding a railroad speeder and a handcar coupled behind. He counted fourteen men. They all clambered off, but only two of them walked down the series of corduroyed walks to the office. There was no mistaking one of them as Croft Brunner, but it took him a while to realize that the soft-looking man at his side was Swiftwater Tilton.

When Tim was attending school at Prince Albert, Tilton had been the town's leading citizen. His mills had been expanding at that time, and as a result a three-year recession in the timber market had struck him harder than most other operators and he'd have failed altogether had not Brunner rescued him. Near failure had left its mark on Tilton. He no longer had an erect, crisp manner. He was heavier, his skin pink and pouchy. He even needed a shave.

Tim stepped outside and shook Tilton's hand. The man exuded an odor of liquor, not the fresh odor of one who has just taken a drink, but the stale hint of saturation. He also exchanged greetings with Brunner, who said: "Tim, I'm glad you're not meeting us with Winchesters. I was afraid of it. We both made fools of ourselves the other night."

"Sure, Tim, sure," Swiftwater kept saying. He followed inside with his watery eyes shifting around the room, apparently in the hope that Tim would produce a bottle, but there was not a drop of liquor in the camp. "That's right, Tim. It wasn't our fault . . . that . . . you know . . ." He meant Clay's death. "I know how it must look to you, Tim, but it was none of our doing."

Tim had no intention of talking about his uncle's killing. He motioned for them to sit down and asked: "What was it you wanted?"

"Business, Tim," Brunner answered. "I was up here a while back and made an offer to Clay, and he turned it down. It was fair, so I'll make the same one to you. I'll pay you seventy thousand dollars for the timber you own north of the Granite Knob. That will leave you in possession of all you're logging now with the exception of that section above Nokewin Lake. Furthermore, I'll open the railroad, and you can have as much time as you want settling for those repairs."

The abruptness of the offer was a surprise. Any such amount as $70,000 was a surprise, too. Tim Chipman stood up and took a turn around the room. He stopped and met Brunner's eyes. "Our holdings north of the Knob aren't worth that much and you know it."

"Is that an objection?"

"No. I just wondered why you offered it."

"I buy for the future. More than that, I'm sorry for everything that's happened. I was partly in the wrong about your dad and Clay. And there's Lynne. She doesn't like this fighting. We're going to be married, you know . . ."

Chipman's expression showed nothing. He was like all the other Chipmans when he had the black mood about him. His face would go blank with a high-boned look, and his voice would be soft as buckskin. "Let's stick to business."

"Well, if it would hurt your conscience to take seventy thousand, I could lower it to fifty."

"It would never hurt my conscience to take money away from you, Brunner. We'll leave it at seventy thousand."

"And you'll sign?"

"I'll think it over."

"Until when?"

"I'll think it over."

After they had gone, Tim Chipman went through the books again. There was no reason for Brunner's offer. He thought about it all afternoon, and about sundown he took a handcar from the company sheds and pumped it along the curving tracks to the Talka barricade. One of the guards had been there the night before; the other was a stranger. He asked for directions to Swiftwater Tilton's house, and was told he'd probably find the man down at the company building.

"With Brunner?" he asked casually.

"I doubt it."

That was all the information he got, but evidently Brunner had gone somewhere. It was dark by then. Light made a ruddy glow against the windows of the big room. He walked past the company store with no one paying the least attention. He stepped to the porch of the company house, looked in a side window.

160

Swiftwater Tilton stood facing the fire, smoking a pipe. He hadn't lighted the lamp, and most of the room was in shadow. A bottle and glass stood on the table behind him. Evidently he'd just had a drink. Tim could not be certain, but he didn't think there was anyone else in the room.

He entered without knocking and stood in the archway a moment, looking across the room before Tilton realized he was there.

"Tim!" His voice had a different sound when Brunner was not around. He walked across, and shook his head. "I'm glad to see you, Tim."

"Brunner around?"

"He went . . . somewhere. Tim . . . concerning that offer . . . that's what you came down here about, wasn't it?"

"In a way. I wanted to know why he was getting to be so generous."

The question made Tilton nervous. He opened the bottle and managed to pour a drink without spilling any. He slid the bottle over for Tim and, without waiting, downed the liquor in his glass. It seemed to help him.

He laughed, and there was a bitter sound in it. "Croft has never been noted for his generosity, that's true. I want to be honest with you, Tim. I want you to know the truth. Don't ever let him know I told you this, but what he's really after is that High Chilkao grant, north of the Granite Knob."

Tim Chipman looked perplexed. He was familiar with the High Chilkao. It was a stand of white pine unrivaled in the North, but according to stipulations in the grant when first awarded to the old Fitzhugh Company, none of it could be cut for a period of 100 years. Thirty years before, the elder Fitzhugh had thrown it in on a sawmill deal he'd made with Tim's grandfather. Considerable time had passed, but it was still fifty years away from the hungry saws of Brunner's mill. He started to say as much, but Swiftwater stopped him.

"Listen. Did you ever hear of the British Columbian Lands Act that Sir Leonard Tilley shoved through to placate the British Columbian interests after the first failure of the Canadian Pacific Railway? There was a clause in that bill which limited all so-called Crown restrictions to fifty years. It was passed to free certain islands along the coast for the salmon interests, but four tracts of timber were included by accident. Two of them were destroyed by the great fire of Eighteen Eighty-Nine. Another is a chunk of white pine protected by the National Parks Law. Don't ask me how Brunner found out it could be interpreted to include the Chilkao. But it can."

"You mean it could be cut now?"

"Actually the time expired two years ago."

Tim whistled softly. "And how much is it really worth?"

"To Brunner? It would make his Talka River Company the biggest outfit north of the Chilkoos. To you, I can't see that the timber is worth much of anything."

Tim Chipman was thoughtful for a while. "I'm not so sure."

"You have no way of logging it. Believe me . . . all this trouble hasn't come about by accident. Brunner has you bottled and the cork driven in."

"Even if I raised my share on the railroad?"

"Then he'd find something else. You'd better sell. I've always liked you, Tim. Pat was my friend, and Clay, too, until a year ago. I don't want to see you go out of here with nothing but the bundle on your back."

"Or in a pine box like Clay. He said no, too, didn't he?"

"You think Brunner killed him."

"Not Brunner. He'd have Ole do it."

"Croft Brunner is no murderer, and neither is that dumb Swede. I'll admit Croft's tough and headstrong. He'll tramp over people to get his way. But he's not a murderer. No matter what Ole blabbed the other night, he's not a murderer. Listen, Tim. Clay had trouble inside his own camp."

"Who with?"

"That's up to you to find out. I'll not accuse anyone without proof."

Tim looked in his eyes. They were red, and watery, and perhaps a trifle frightened, but he was telling the truth, or thought he was.

Swiftwater said: "Take that seventy thousand, Tim. Take it and buy in on that new pulp mill in Prince Albert. Pulp is the future of this country. If you still hate Brunner, you can grow with that industry and fight him . . ."

"I'd like to look at that High Chilkao timber first." He'd spoken the words softly, but there was something in his tone that brought a sharp glance from Swiftwater Tilton.

"You sounded just like old Pat then. Well, forget about it. I don't know why I ever supposed a Chipman would be anything but a Chipman."

They talked about other things. A man wearing hobnailed boots walked around the porch, and both of them recognized the stride to be Brunner's. He came in and drew up suddenly when he saw Tim Chipman by the fire. Then he walked on, showing his strong teeth in a smile.

"Well, Tim. I hope you decided to make a poor man of me."

"I don't want to sell the High Chilkao."

Brunner seemed to flinch when the words hit him. He glanced at Tilton, and back at Tim. Then he shrugged, and turned as was his habit to warm his hands at the fire. "I thought I was the only man in the North who knew the time limit on that pine had expired. How did you find out?"

"I read minds."

"You must. Well, what do you plan to do . . . log it?"

"Yes."

"You're a fool, Chipman. If anyone but me had made you the offer, you'd have taken it. But you hate me. You've hated me ever since the night I flattened your father across that campfire down on the Rouge. Leave your emotions out of it and be a businessman for a while. That High Chilkao pine isn't worth five hundred dollars to anyone except me, because I'm the only one who can log it."

"You're not going to log it, Brunner."

"No?" Brunner's lips were pulled tight, revealing his teeth in a savage smile. His fists were doubled and there was a sag to his shoulders like there'd been the instant before he'd smashed Ole down the other night. He was probably tempted to give Tim some of the same, but he conquered it and let his shoulders jerk in a laugh. "Maybe you intend to log it?"

"You guessed right, I intend to log it."

"Go ahead. But when your logs are sawed and bucked, you may have to wait a few days for the train. You might even have to wait a few years."

"Then they'll rot on the ground and I'll sell the knots for firewood."

"That's a dog-in-the-manger attitude!"

"You're a self-made man, Brunner. You wouldn't want to ride into the millionaire class on a Chipman's back."

Brunner ignored the thrust. "I'll make it eighty thousand for that timber!"

"No."

Brunner took a deep breath and the bulge of his shoulders relaxed. He was good at controlling himself when he had to. He even managed a laugh. "All right, Tim, then I'll get it for nothing."

CHAPTER
FOUR

Tim Chipman had a look at the High Chilkao timber, then he called a stop on his other operations and brought his bosses in to the home camp for a meeting. Those on hand were old Ole Halseth, who was known by no other name than Ole Olsen, Dick Poole, Lefty Johnson, and Steve Riika.

Tim marked the limits of the tract on a large-scale map on the wall and said: "First thing we'll do is build a road up there. We'll get the timber out, all right." He spent half an hour on details, then turned to Dick Poole and said: "I understand there's someone in your camp telling the boys I won't be able to meet the next payroll."

Dick Poole was only five feet eight or nine, but his thickness and breadth made him a big man. He'd been fidgety all the while, and mention of trouble in his camp brought a flush of anger beneath his dark-burned skin. "Clay never had any fault to find with my camp."

"Don't get on the prod, Dick. If there's somebody up there spreading yarns for Brunner, I want to know about it."

"Brunner's got nobody staked out in my camp." He looked over at Steve Riika as though he expected to be contradicted, but Steve didn't say anything. He cooled off a little. "You know how men talk. There's always them that'll grumble about the bosses." He met Tim's gaze. "Maybe there is a chance you won't meet some pay days!"

"We'll pay off."

"I never said you wouldn't," Poole muttered.

After the meeting broke up, Steve asked: "You think Brunner's got men up in that camp stirrin' things up?"

"Of course. Brunner wouldn't pass a chance like that."

Next morning Tim set out with one pack horse and a couple of helpers to cruise the High Chilkao. Night found them camped in deep timber on the Ouragan, one of the forks of Mad River. It was a wild country there, untouched by the axe. Mist had descended and there were a few drifting flakes of snow. The snow increased during the night and they woke up to find their tent sagging under its weight.

After a breakfast of flapjacks and bacon they packed and went on, skirting the high ridge of the Granite Knob and doubling back to strike the Chilkao from the west side. Tim Chipman walked ahead by himself and stood with his back to one of the forest giants. There was scarcely any underbrush, and the huge trunks were widely spaced, rising straight as pillars in a Grecian temple. Most of the stand had reached maturity, and the trees were unusually uniform in size. They rose from brace roots broader than a man's outflung arms and tapered quickly to a trunk that rose without a

167

branch to a remote height before the top spread out toward the sky.

Winter birds had been raising a chatter, hunting seeds that had fallen on the new snow, but once inside the High Chilkao there was silence. It had a primeval quality, as though it had always existed and always would. It combined and became a part of the forest, making him feel insignificant. It seemed preposterous that a little thing like man could, in a few years, flatten such a forest and leave it an ugly chaos of stumps and branches. He knew then that he would never let the High Chilkao go. Brunner would never get a saw into it — and neither would he. The fringe, perhaps, the small timber at the southern edge, some of the giants that had reached old age — but the rest would stand as it was. It is a fallacy that a forest needs to be laid flat in order to make lumber. He'd stood longer than he realized, and finally the thud of horses' hoofs across snow-dusted pine needles caught his attention. It was dark when they once again touched the Ouragan, a small stream here with thin ice forming along its infrequent backwaters.

Next day they followed a rough compass bearing true south, pausing during mid-afternoon on a crest of the Granite Knob. The sun was shining, thawing the snow. He could see the headquarters camp some nine or ten miles away. At his left rose a thin streak of smoke marking Ole Olsen's steam donkey-engine where saw logs were still being yarded in the fading anticipation that sometime the railroad would be opened to Vermilion. In the other direction the Granite Knob diminished in size and became rolling hills, breaking off suddenly in the deep-gashed gulches near Mad River Cañon.

From his vantage point he could see that it was an even slant along side hills all the way to Mad River. The distance was not more than eleven miles, and a rail line could be built along it without encountering a major obstacle. It happened that there was almost that exact length of line lying disused between his main camp and the Talka River's main boundary. The possibility of escaping from Brunner's trap by ripping up that useless segment and laying it to the Mad River had been growing in his mind for several days. The Mad was a rocky and treacherous stream, and throughout most of the year it could be used only to float logs of pulping size, but the spring breakup could be depended on to give at least four days of high water and carry his winter cut to Beaver Lake, thence to be rafted to the mills of either the Beaver or the Macardle Company, where such clear quality pine would command the usual premium.

After two more days spent mapping the Chilkao Grant, Tim Chipman returned to the headquarters camp and called a meeting of his bosses to explain his plan. He took some pains to mark the projected rail line across a large-scale contour map on the wall.

Poole said: "I think it's a good way to end up with an axe handle between the eyes. If you think Brunner's going to stand for tearing up that rail line of his . . ."

"Maybe he'll get an axe handle between *his* eyes."

"Listen, you know Brunner. He'll be shoved just so far . . ."

"You can shove a Chipman just so far, too."

Poole clamped his mouth shut and sat back in surly silence.

"It bane good idea, all right," Olsen said after some consideration. "But rails ain't goin' to do any good wit'out engine and cars. Cars, anyhow. Aye suppose you could coast full cars down grade and use horses to pull empty ones back. But . . ."

"I'll get a train."

"Yah. Maybe you bane order from Monkey Ward?"

"I'll get it from Brunner. He's running three trains. By rights one of them is mine. Tomorrow morning at ten o'clock one of them will be starting back from the Landing. It'll have a crew of four. They won't make much trouble. We'll board it at the head of Wolverine Gulch. I want a half dozen men to go down there with me, and about that many waiting in the jack spruce just above Brunner's barricade."

Ole jumped to his feet and beat the pitch-hardened legs of his tin pants. "By golly, yah. Aye goin' down there and whip five, sax Brunner men myself. For long time noo Aye bane needin' geude fight."

"We'll get fight enough out of him, but not tomorrow. If things go right, we'll have that train up there before Brunner knows what's happened. Steve, I want you to have a crew ready to pull rails. After we get a few hundred yards of it torn up, there's not much he can do."

Ole selected ten men, mostly Swedes and old-timers on the Chipman payroll. He asked: "How about Winchester guns? Some of the boys . . ."

"We'll let Brunner do the shooting. Maybe the time will come for us to go down there blasting, but I don't think it'll be tomorrow. You tell the boys to take along a few axe handles. They'll be enough."

Ole went out, leaving him alone.

Tim sat at the big, rough-board table where his father had once liked to sit. Beneath the kerosene hanging lamp he looked gaunt and rangy. Old Pat had wanted to leave a timber empire for his son. Tim was thinking about the way in which things had turned themselves around, and that he was trying to save the company more in his father's memory than for himself. He wouldn't be beaten by the same man who had smashed his father down that night at the mouth of the Rouge.

Wolves were howling, and there were the sharper barks of coyotes riding clearly through the sharp air. The fire had gone out, but he was not cold in his heavy flannel shirt and blanket-lined trousers. He stood up and walked to the water bucket. A thin shell of ice was freezing over it. Each night the thermometer had been dropping a little nearer the zero mark. It would be ten above before morning. Winter and the big freeze were not far away. He had some work to do, pulling rails and ties, leveling ground and cutting underbrush, before the ground was frozen rock-hard, although the actual laying of track didn't worry him. There are worse surfaces than frozen ground and packed snow.

171

He broke the ice and had a drink from the lip of the bucket. He went back to his old place and sat down. An hour passed while he half closed his eyes and visualized each segment of railroad from Vermilion to the barricade, planning every small move of the next morning's work.

A dog was barking somewhere with repeated insistence. It was old Gyp, the black-and-tan malamute that hung around the cook house. He'd been barking for a considerable time before Tim took notice. A man said something, and the dog quieted to a whimper. It was Jim Mahon's voice. Jim was the guard who had stopped him with a Winchester on his arrival ten days before.

Boots thudded outside, the door opened, and Mahon thrust his head in: "There's a girl here, Tim."

Tim walked to the door and saw that it was Lynne Tilton. Her face seemed a little bit frightened.

"Says she's alone," Mahon added.

"It's all right."

Mahon hesitated an instant and withdrew. Lynne came inside, closing the door after her. She stood for a while, leaning her shoulders against it, looking up at Tim's face.

"I'd just as soon nobody knew I was here," she said.

"Mahon won't talk."

She took time to dust some flakes of new-fallen snow off her Mackinaw. Then she unbuttoned it and walked to the stove.

He could see a shudder pass through her slim body. "I'll build a fire."

"Never mind. I can only stay a moment."

He waited for her to give the reason for her visit. She had a hard time commencing.

"I had to come and tell you, Tim. They know what you plan to do tomorrow morning. About boarding the train. You mustn't try it."

It jolted him for a moment that Brunner knew. Then he laughed. "You found out almost as soon as I did. Brunner's pigeon must have a fast pair of legs. What has he got cooked up for me?"

"I don't know. Tim, don't think badly of Croft. You know how things have always been out here. A thing like you plan has always meant war, and in a timber war . . ."

"In other words, he figured on having his boys out there with Winchesters."

"Don't say it like that!" There was a ring of defense in her voice. She went on: "Croft isn't a killer, if that's what you mean . . ."

"No. You wouldn't marry him if you thought he was. So you keep telling yourself he isn't. Well, maybe you're right. I don't know who let Clay have it in the head."

"It wasn't Croft!"

Tim laughed. There was a bitter sound to it.

"Why did you laugh like that?"

"I was thinking of . . . things. About your being engaged to marry Brunner, and coming out here to warn me when it might mean winning or losing the things Brunner wants more than anything else in the world."

"I didn't come here any more for your sake than for his. I don't want him to have blood on his hands."

"There's nothing to stop me from keeping you here and changing my plans . . . do you realize that?"

"You wouldn't do it, Tim!"

"Brunner would do it."

She didn't answer. She knew it was the truth. She knew, as everyone else knew, how Croft Brunner hated the Chipmans and would do anything to win.

Tim went on: "Well, that's the difference between Brunner and me. He sees what he wants and takes it. I'm not just talking about timber."

She'd moved across the room. Now she stood with her back to the table, looking up at him. Excitement showed in the quick rise and fall of her breast. Winter had heightened the color in her cheeks, but there was an added flush now. She said: "If you think I was part of his winnings from my father . . ."

"Of course not. Maybe you're in love with him. He's good-looking. He has money. He's a man."

"I do love him, Tim. I care a good deal for him."

"Sure."

She knew he didn't believe her. She went on: "No one has ever been as good to me as Croft. There're two sides to him, Tim. There's a side that's rough and merciless. I know that. But there's another side . . ."

"That makes him be generous to his conquests."

"You mean me. And my father . . ."

"Oh, no. He didn't win you in a timber war. Not directly. But men like to think of women as conquests. I'd like to think of you as one of my conquests, too."

"Tim." She spoke his name in a negative way, as though to check him from going on.

"I'll tell you something, Lynne. Maybe you guessed it. I've heard women are good at such things. When we were kids back at Prince Albert, I used to spend half my time thinking about you, but I wouldn't have the nerve to speak to you when I met you in the hall at school. Then I went away, and after a while I got over it. Or thought I did. Months would go by and I'd hardly think of you, until maybe I saw someone who did something that reminded me of you, and there the old pain would be, as bad as ever. Yes, I'll call it a pain, because that's what it was. Then I woke up in that bunk at Talka and looked up and saw you. Everything came back. The three or four years didn't mean a thing. When I found out you were going to marry Croft Brunner, I hated him. Maybe that's why I'm fighting him. I don't know. I've never analyzed it. But I'm into it now, and I'm going to keep on fighting him. I'm going to whip him, Lynne. I'm going to beat him for that High Chilkao timber, and for the railroad. And maybe even for you."

She was standing with her back to the table, arms straight at her sides, her hands clenched. His words had left her a trifle open-eyed. Even though she'd known all along, his admission amazed her. "Tim, you should have said something, before . . ."

"This isn't too late."

He took a step forward, grabbed her by the shoulders. She made no move to escape. For a space of half a dozen seconds they looked in each other's eyes. Then he drew her hard against him.

She moved then, trying to twist away, but her strength was nothing in comparison with his.

"Lynne!" he said.

"Let me go," she whispered. "This will only make it worse."

"You don't want me to let you go."

"Of course, I do. I'm going to marry Croft. What you said doesn't change anything."

She didn't finish what she started to say. Instead, she went on with something almost like a sob in her voice: "Oh, Tim. If you'd come a year ago. Six months ago . . ."

"I told you I'm not too late."

She shook her head. She'd forced her hands between them and was pushing herself away. He let go of her shoulders.

"I'm sorry, Lynne. It took a lot for you to come up here. I guess I don't sound as though I appreciated it very much. I do. For Croft Brunner's sake, I'll see to it that I don't get killed."

"You mean you won't try to take the train?"

He shrugged his shoulders. It could have meant anything. There was an uncomfortable silence. She broke it to say: "I'll have to go. They might miss me, and . . ."

"I'll go along. Wait a moment."

Tim went to his room, wrote a hurried note for Steve Riika, found Clay's old Enfield revolver, and thrust it beneath his belt, dumped a box of fifty cartridges in his Mackinaw pocket. Then he buttoned his Mackinaw over the gun and walked out.

Lynne Tilton was waiting for him near the door.

176

CHAPTER
FIVE

It was snowing lightly, and as always during winter nights in that country there was a slight mist. Tim stopped at the bunkhouse with the message for Riika, then he walked with Lynne down a forest pathway to the canoe deck. He was sure no one but Mahon had seen her.

A couple of canoes were upended on the dock. He broke shell ice and dumped one into the water. The girl knew how to use a canoe paddle. She crouched on her knees in near the bow, helping guide the craft with confident strokes.

The Talka was a swift stream, dark-flowing between snowy shores. Here and there it broke unexpectedly into riffles or plunged in short stretches of rapids. After traveling for almost half an hour in silence, Tim spoke a word or two, and she helped him bring the canoe up through shallow water.

"You're coming?" she asked, her voice sounding surprised to find that he'd followed her to shore.

"There's some spruce down here I've been wanting to measure."

She knew he was joking. "I wish I knew what was on your mind. When I was a little girl, Dad warned me that all Chipmans were crazy."

Tim laughed. It was an easy sound, with all the taut anger gone from his voice.

She said: "Don't gamble on getting that train, Tim. Promise me you won't."

She'd stopped and was facing him. It was dense black beneath the spruce trees, with snowflakes appearing suddenly as gray streaks around them. He could picture her face without seeing it. He was aware of the warmth of her breath, the forest fragrance of her hair.

He said: "I'll not start anything I can't finish."

"There's nothing more I can say."

He knew what she thought — that he'd go ahead with his plans anyway.

They walked together along a game trail, finding their way by woodsman's instinct more than through sense of sight. Unexpectedly the lights of Talka Camp appeared in white and yellowish blurs through mist and falling snow.

"Good bye," she said, and without hesitation turned and hurried away through foggy darkness.

He stood for a while listening to the whisper of her boots in the snow. At last he turned and picked his way back toward the river.

A boom of cable-anchored logs made an uncertain bridge that bobbed beneath his weight as he crossed the half-frozen millpond. Men were working with pike poles, breaking logs loose for the next morning's mill feed. Tim was soon out of sight in forest along the bottoms.

A slight grayness was hinting at dawn when he came in sight of Vermilion Landing. He made a circle of the camp, crossed the railroad. A phone wire leading from the trading post to Talka Camp was strung along the trunks of jack-spruce trees parallel to the tracks. He climbed one of the trees to break it. The job took a couple of minutes, bending wire back and forth until it was hot in his hands. He tore down fifty feet of it, coiled the wire, and threw it far up the hillside. Then he circled along the tree-covered slope and seated himself on a deadfall to look at the scene below.

The train was there, as he'd expected, standing by the loading sheds. Steam was up, the smokestack and valves making ascending clouds that disintegrated in the sharp morning air.

Ten or twelve minutes passed. Finally a man walked along the line of unloaded flatcars carrying a lantern he no longer needed, and went inside the little overnight shack where the train crew stayed. In a few seconds, sparks and new smoke came from the stovepipe, showing he'd poked up the fire.

It looked easy. Tim slid downhill through leafless buck brush and juniper, followed the railroad ditch for a few yards, and reached the side of the engine. It was a small locomotive, made for power rather than speed. No one was in the cab. He climbed the two steps. Pine knots were hissing in the firebox and he knew by the sound of the valves that a good head of steam was up. The gauge stood at eighty-five pounds.

He heard the creak of cold-constricted hinges as the door to the shack opened. A man said something to

179

those inside, and closed the door. Tim watched him cross a couple sets of side tracks, coming toward the engine. He was a short, dark-whiskered man, wearing a dirty blue Mackinaw and Scotch cap.

Tim remained quite still, but aside from that he made no particular effort to conceal himself. The whiskered man climbed to the cab and drew up suddenly. Tim had drawn the Enfield and was aiming it hip high.

"What the devil?"

Tim spoke: "You know what this thing is. It's a gun. I don't want to pull the trigger, and I don't think I'll have to." He had no intention of pulling the trigger, but the whiskered man didn't know that. Fear was clawing inside him and his eyes showed it.

"What do you want?" he managed to whisper.

"We're going to Chipman."

"But . . ."

"We're going to Chipman. Now."

"You can't get through to Chipman," the whiskered man worked up nerve enough to say. "They got the track barricaded."

"I'll worry about that. You get this thing to moving."

"Sure. Just keep that gun to yourself."

The whiskered man eased on the throttle and the engine responded with a sudden jerk as it broke its wheels free from frost. Couplings banged to the end of the train, but for the moment nobody had appeared in the door of the shack.

"Get it going," Tim hissed between his teeth.

180

The whiskered man cast another glance at the gun and gave it more steam. Slowly they picked up speed. The door of the shack flew open and a man stood in the opening, pants in one hand, dressed only in a flannel shirt and long underwear.

"Hey, what's the idea, there . . . ?"

"Tell him it's all right."

The black-whiskered man leaned from the engine as if to obey, but at the final second he saw that the gun muzzle was not pointed at him, and he leaped.

"Chipman!" he shouted. "It's Tim Chipman!"

Others ran outside. One of them had a rifle. He tossed it up and fired. Tim saw the red pencil of flame in the half darkness, and an instant later the clang of its high velocity slug glanced from engine steel. The man remained in the door, half hidden, working the gun lever, firing the magazine dry. A bullet struck somewhere amid pipes leading to the gauges, its soft nose leaving a streak like silver. Bits of metal stung Chipman's cheek. He stayed down, hearing other bullets glance from the cab, from the flat side of the tender. Seven shots in all. He looked over the wood-heaped tender. Two men were running across the side tracks trying to catch the last car.

Tim fired and saw the bullet strike where he'd aimed it, kicking up a geyser of dirt and snow ten feet in front of them. One of them fell as though hit. He was the man with the rifle. It skidded away from him. He rolled to his stomach, grabbed the rifle, aimed from the ground, but there was no sound. It was evidently empty. The other man could have reached the last car, but he lost his stomach for it and headed down the track. Another rifle commenced whanging from the shack window, but the distance was rapidly building up between them.

A speeder was ready in the tool house and they might be able to catch him, but he doubted that they would. First thing they'd do would be rush down to use Burgess's telephone. He'd be halfway to Talka before they decided what to do next.

Increasing grade slowed the engine. He made the head of Wolverine Gulch, rolled around some little basaltic cliffs, and across a broad divide. After that it was almost level going. The little engine put on speed until it weaved crazily along the narrow track. There was dawn without sun, a bright grayness with the forest around him quickly dissolving in fog. The engine made a final curve and burst through timber above the Talka Camp. He could see the larger buildings and the ruddy flare of waste burners, but most of the camp was rendered uncertain by fog.

He'd have to stop for the switch. He cut the throttle and brought the engine to a stop with its iron brake shoes whining.

He'd misjudged and was forty or fifty feet short of the switch. He leaped from the cab, ran to it, swung the lever. It was fouled by dirt and snow and he had to bring the lever down repeatedly before it would close.

A bullet rattled half-frozen gravel three of four yards away, and an instant later came a distant crack of a rifle. It was a long way off, 300 yards or more. Back in the engine cab he caught sight of a man running from

182

one of the houses, carrying a rifle in one hand. The man didn't try to shoot again.

He had the train moving, rapidly picking up speed. Momentarily the camp was out of sight beyond tool sheds. He had another glimpse of Talka before the timber closed in. Men were standing outside the bunkhouses, apparently watching him.

Another half mile would bring him to the barricade. He pulled the whistle cord for three long blasts — the signal he'd arranged with Steve Riika. He wasn't at all sure they'd be there to attack and knock down the barricade. He thought he heard the sound of shooting, but he couldn't be certain amid the ringing clatter of wheels and couplings.

The road burst from timber and followed a rocky side hill. He grabbed the whistle cord again — stopped. The sound of gunfire was close ahead.

Mist was heavier there, along the hills. Successive layers of fog whipped around the engine. Sometimes he could see ten yards ahead, sometimes fifty. He recognized a lightning-blackened spruce that hung at an angle over the track and knew the barricade was only fifty yards ahead. Fog faded and he glimpsed it — still intact.

A man was in the track waving a rifle over his head, signaling the train to stop. He was a big fellow, one of the guards who had been with Ole that first night. Tim couldn't have stopped the engine if he'd wanted to. The man plunged headlong from the track, picked himself up, and clawed his way up the steep approach of hillside.

A rifle bullet whanged engine metal. Tim lay on the floor. He waited for the crash of the barricade. It seemed to take a long time. A voice shouted, apparently right beside him. Then there was a rip and splinter. Not loud, as he'd expected. He was vaguely aware of timbers whisking the air outside the cab. The engine was still clattering, careening up the track. He couldn't resist a whoop of elation. He was safely through.

He stood up. Fog had already closed, hiding him from Brunner's men. He eased up on the throttle. It had been a long time since the Chipman segment of track had been attended to.

Halfway to the camp he met Bob Marr with a crew of fifteen men, pushing a flatcar loaded with sledges and spike pullers. He took them aboard and backed slowly to the Chipman south boundary. He heard guns still hammering in the fog.

"Ole and his Swedes," Bob Marr said.

Ole Olsen had taken his boys there heeled, after all. Perhaps it was lucky, although Tim didn't want a bullet put through a Brunner man on Brunner's ground. Like all log operators in that wild Northwest timber, Brunner liked to settle things without calling on the law, but he'd do it if he thought it would mean an advantage.

"This is where we start," Tim said, stopping the last car at a tree blaze marking the start of Talka ground.

He got down and walked to the last car. No shooting now. He could hear voices in the fog. It gave him an eerie feeling, like hearing a voice detached from a body. It was daylight, but no sign of the sun.

The crew commenced tearing up track, and for the next quarter hour there were no sounds except the steady creaking of spike pullers, the grate and thud as spikes and rail plates were flung in the flatcar.

"Hey, there!" a voice called. It was Steve Riika.

Tim told him to come down.

"Holy Mackinaw . . . you pullin' track already?"

"We got to work fast while the fog holds. How many men do you have?"

"Machi and Mahon are with me. Olsen's up there with his Swedes. Twelve of 'em, unless somebody ran into a slug."

"What kind of a fight did you have?"

"Fight? . . . Hah! What fight you have when nobody can see gunsights in fog? We might as well have shot blank. Why don't you let us know you comin' quicker? We don't have time for barricade."

"Forget it, Steve. I wanted the fun of smashing it down."

Additional men came down from camp. Ole Olsen and his Swedes were there, too. The train was almost constantly in motion, withdrawing, reeling in the track after it.

CHAPTER
SIX

The fog was lifting. From his place atop the last flatcar, Tim Chipman saw the arrival of men at Brunner's south boundary. He sprang down and walked that way to meet them.

"Stay behind," he said, when Steve Riika commenced to follow.

He stopped after covering half the distance and waited as a man shoved his way through the Talka gang. Croft Brunner. Tim knew him instantly by the confident swing of his body. For a second Tim thought he was coming alone, then Axe-Handle Ole, huge as an upright grizzly bear, slogged after him.

Brunner kept walking until only a half dozen steps separated them. He stopped, legs spread, hands on his hips, his face looking dark and heavy-jawed. "Under the laws of this country you've just committed armed assault and robbery. Do you think I'm going to let you get away with it?"

"All right. We'll turn it over to the officials at Prince Albert. We'll drop the rest of the business into their laps, too. Your monopoly of this railroad, for instance."

"No, Chipman. I'm not going to call on the law. There's a law older than those Ottawa statutes in this country. It's the law that every timber concern is ruler of its own ground. You came on my ground this morning and stole my property. And now I'm coming to take it back."

"That'll be quite a trick . . . running that train without rails."

"I give you warning . . ."

"You've given me enough warning. Get off my land."

The words were like a blow across Brunner's face. A flush mounted beneath his deep tan, and muscles thickened under his Mackinaw. He cursed through set teeth and lunged forward. He had a looseness in his shoulders that Tim had seen the night he had flattened Axe-Handle Ole.

Tim knew better than to take the full shocking power of those sledgehammer fists, but instead of retreating he came forward half a step. Brunner had started a left. It glanced from the side of Tim's head. Tim knew the other fist was coming close after it. He dropped his left elbow, caught the force of the blow, shifted, and smashed a right of his own — a short punch that caught Brunner at the base of his ribs, just beneath the heart. It jolted him and made him stagger back. Tim was after him in the same instant, trying to grab the advantage. But Brunner was merely knocked off balance. He was bent and twisted partly away. He timed the move and came around. Tim had no chance to check himself. He twisted and rode with the fist. Even so it had a stunning effect, like being struck by a club.

He was dully conscious of being down amid rough gravel and snow of the torn-up roadbed. He realized Brunner was coming to trample him beneath his hobnailed boots. He was able to move in time. The heavy boot whipped across his Mackinaw. He caught it against his chest, lunged to his feet while Brunner fought to get free. For a second Brunner was on one foot, clutching Tim's Mackinaw. Then he sprawled on back and shoulder.

Axe-Handle Ole had been crouched over, watching. A roar of delight had come from his throat when Tim had hit the gravel, but now that his boss was down, his shout turned to anger, and he sprang forward, swinging the axe handle for the side of Tim Chipman's neck.

Tim saw him and was able to fling himself out of the way. The footing was bad. He slipped, and fell down the abrupt four feet of railroad grade. Ole started to follow, and checked himself. Steve Riika had been running up the tracks swinging an axe handle of his own, and Ole had to turn to meet him.

Other men were coming on the run, men from both sides. By the time Tim Chipman got to his feet, the battle was a wild mix-up around him. He saw Mahon slug a man to the ground. Axe-Handle Ole was bellowing, charging through Chipman men, swinging the axe handle in mighty arcs.

"Coom on, you tank you whip Axe-Handle Ole!"

A man had fallen. Ole Olsen, the yard boss. Axe-Handle was about to stamp over him, but Olsen stood up. Axe-Handle tried to hurl him aside with his left hand, but the yard boss clinched. The unexpected

188

fury of Ole Olsen's attack made Axe-Handle Ole stagger to catch his balance. It gave Olsen the chance he wanted, and he rammed his forked fingers upward to the huge man's eyes.

Axe-Handle was temporarily blinded. He reeled, bellowed, swung the axe handle. He tripped and fell down the embankment. He was on his face in snow-filled weeds. He got to his feet and groped like a blinded Cyclops.

"Aye make you geude Swede, by golly!" Ole Olsen shouted. "Noo shall Aye split your skull, yah!"

The words found their way to Axe-Handle's brain. He became terrified of what he could not see. He started running at a gargantuan gallop. He tripped and fell, got up, ran again. Sight of Ole in flight took the nerve out of Brunner's gang. Half a dozen started to retreat. Even the curses of Brunner himself could not stop them. The fight stopped as quickly as it started.

Brunner followed them, stopped twenty or thirty paces down the track, shook his fist at Tim Chipman. "That train will never haul logs. I'll stop you. I'll stop you if I have to hire every timber tough in the North!"

Next day, Tim Chipman called in his men from the Nokewin Lake Camp, and stopped all his other operations. He divided the men into three camps — one to pull and lay track, one to build log bunkhouses at the High Chilkao, and a timber crew to start cutting a forty-acre block of white pine at the edge of the grant.

That brought the month near pay-day time, so, to raise money, Tim Chipman portaged a canoe to Mad

River that he followed to Beaver Lake. After eighteen miles along the narrow lake he reached the Beaver Milling Company sawmill, but D. W. Grayson was in Vancouver and his superintendent was without power to make an offer or advance on the next season's cut of timber. So Tim set off again, reaching the Macardle mill about sundown.

Old Man Macardle himself was on hand, roughly clad and begrimed with sawdust. Like most sawmill men, he'd been reduced to cutting the cheaper varieties of wood, and like other independents he experienced trouble in marketing his finished product. White pine would be a different matter, and he chuckled at the anticipation of having lumber buyers standing the drinks for a change. The matter of an advance took some of the pleasure out of it for the Scotsman, but Chipman was an old concern, so he finally relented to an extent necessary for the next month's payroll with some left over for supplies.

It was necessary for Tim to travel on to Prince Albert, returning to his home camp a day later than he'd anticipated, but beneath the pay day deadline. He'd noticed tension in the camp before he left, and now it was worse.

"Somebody been stirring the boys up?" he asked Riika.

Riika shrugged. "You can't stop timber jack from cussin' the boss every night when he sit along deacon seat."

"I might stop the one that tipped off Brunner the night before we grabbed the train."

"Sure, but who? Maybe even me."

"No, Steve. It was somebody who thought I planned to grab it at ten o'clock, not six."

"Maybe some friend of Ole's. Maybe Mahon."

"How about Poole?"

He was the one both of them had been thinking of from the first. Poole's timber crew wasn't doing well. On the fourth day after Tim's return, three of Poole's men came and asked for their time. Tim paid them off in currency. A couple of days later he learned that they'd gone to work at the Talka mills.

That evening he climbed to the string of wall tents that were serving Poole's crew as quarters pending the erection of a bunkhouse. It was evening, and the men were lined up along the deacon seat waiting for grub. They'd been arguing something, and were suddenly silent when they saw him.

"What's the matter, boys?" he asked. "If you have anything on your minds, unload it. You're getting out no more timber than a crew of Siwash squaws."

After an uneasy area of silence, a young timber feller named Clark said: "We're willing to work. It ain't that. But this ain't a decent place for a man to live. I didn't hire out to freeze on some nosebag show . . ."

"Did you hire out as a front-office punk or a timber stiff? A little fall nip won't hurt you. The bunkhouse will be finished in ten days. What else is bothering you?"

"Wages, that's what."

"I just paid you your wages."

"We got it straight you'll never meet another pay day."

"Who told you that?"

Clark was surly and silent.

Tim went on: "Chipman hasn't missed a pay day in thirty years. See that timber back there . . . the High Chilkao? I could sell it any day I wanted for enough to pay your wages through the next ten years. Who told you I wouldn't meet the payroll?"

"I ain't kickin' anybody in the rump. If . . ."

"Maybe your own boss?"

He could feel the tenseness that grabbed every man along the split-log seat when he spoke the words. He knew then it was Poole himself who had been stirring up discontent. He turned, and looked around. Poole had been inside one of the tents, washing his hands. He'd heard what Tim said, but for the moment he was stolid and set-jawed.

"You hear me, Poole?"

"Yah, I heard you." He came from the tent, a broad, powerful man, with little, close-set eyes. He stopped, and killed time by rolling down his sleeves. He saw that everyone was looking at him. He hitched up his trousers. "They ask me things, and I tell 'em the truth. They're my boys. They trust me. I call a spade a —"

"You told them I'd never meet another payroll!"

Poole wanted to deny it. But every man in the camp would have known he was lying and they'd have laid it to cowardice. So he merely stood, truculent and silent.

"Pack your bundle and get out."

"You're firing me? By the Gawd . . ."

192

"Pack your bundle and get out."

Poole spun and looked at the roughly clad timber jacks along the deacon seat. "You goin' to let him git away with this? I been playing along with you boys and here I am gettin' shagged because I was honest with you. How about it? Let's show this school punk. Let's pack our bundles and shake his nosebag show. Let's go down where we can sleep in a bunk and eat offen a table. I got it there's jobs for every stiff that wants one down at the Talka Camp."

There was no way Tim could stop him without making the situation worse. A couple timber jacks jumped up and one of them said: "Now you're talkin'. I'm blowin' this show. I'm through with cold beans and spruce mattresses."

Others got up. Finally eleven were on their feet. Nineteen men were still seated. "Ain't gettin' out. Ain't quittin'. Bane work har here year and Chipman treated me good," a Norwegian by the name of Hanson said. "Ain't workin' alongside that mean Axe-Handle Ole."

Dick Poole said: "Maybe you'd rather work for nothing."

Tim took a long stride and faced him: "Don't say that again."

Poole had hoped to lead the entire camp away with him. When it appeared that almost two-thirds would stay, it angered him. His anger blazed now. He turned and without warning leaped, swung a hobnailed logger boot toward Tim's groin.

Tim side-stepped and smashed him to the ground.

193

Poole rolled and lay on his side for a while. Blood started running from the lower corner of his mouth. He pushed himself on one arm and wiped his lips with the back of his other hand.

"I'll get you for that, Chipman."

"Get me now while I'm handy."

Poole crawled back until there were six or seven steps between them before climbing to his feet.

Tim turned and looked up and down the deacon seat. "Any more of you? If you have any idea to get out, I want you to do it now. It'd be a yellow trick to walk out on me after the big snow blows."

A raw-boned young man with bristly red hair spoke from the ranks of those who had lined up by Poole: "Give it to me straight, Tim. You really think you can pay off?"

"I'll pay every cent."

"That's good enough for me." He went back over and sat on his old place on the deacon seat. When Poole got ready to go, there were only nine men with him. They formed a silent, glowering crowd as they walked along the snow-packed trail to headquarters camp nine miles away.

Departure of the malcontents cleared the air, and during the weeks of early winter a man could sense the new spirit of things at the camps. Timber was cut and bucked and yarded with a speed to match the booming advance of the railroad from Chilkao to Mad River Cañon.

The last spike had been driven for three days when the big blizzard howled down from the north. It lasted a week, leaving the country heaped with two feet of snow and the air sharp from twenty below.

Things settled down to the winter routine. It was the time for cutting timber, for skidding logs down chutes glazed with hot water that turned to ice. There was little rough country or undergrowth in the High Chilkao, making the tract easy to timber. Railroad cars were loaded, and a steady grade all the way to Mad River Cañon allowed them to be run by gravity two or three at a time with men at the hand brakes. Each day the engine was called on only once to haul the empties back.

Once delivered at cañon edge, the logs were not immediately dropped over the steep side. Temporarily they were stacked by means of a small skidder, and Machi, a tall, lean Finlander, knocked the tops from the two huge Douglas spruce trees, one on each side of the cañon, and fitted them with loops for guy cables so a high lead could be stretched. The lead would allow logs to be lowered without the splintering and tangle that might result in a disastrous jam when the Mad thawed out next spring.

It was the second week of December. Tim Chipman was supervising the job of swinging the high cable across the cañon. It was tough at thirty below with frost settling in the bull block, setting up a howling friction that fought the cable.

When he came down after a third trip aloft, a kid from the home camp was waiting for him. It was Buster Dibble, the cook's helper. Buster's scared expression made Tim laugh.

"Fire away, Buster. Has Brunner burned us out?"

"A Mountie's come for you."

"If any Mounted Policeman came to take me away, I dare say I'd find it out from him." He took time to twist up a cigarette from strong Peerless tobacco. One of those Peerless cigarettes would have flattened him two months before, but a man gets to taking things around a timber spread. "What did he say?"

"He wants to see you. The crumb boss gave him coffee and shagged me out the back way. I come the whole way since . . ."

"You're a good boy, Buster, but I got nothing to hide from a Mountie. Not even an engine and a string of cars. We'll get along back there."

They struck off through timber on snowshoes. Winter darkness settled early. There was a long, sunless twilight as afternoon graded into gray evening. Then stars came out, looking like white flares through the mist. Hours passed with no sound except the slight creak of snowshoes. Tim had had a hard day, and a fatigue-like drug settled in his legs when he finally loosened the lashings of his bear-paw webs and walked down a packed pathway to the company house.

There was a light inside, and new steam on the windows told Chipman a fire was going. Ice had locked the door. He bucked it open with his shoulder.

A Mounted Policeman had been sitting with his boots thrust at the stove, reading a paper-backed novel that had been in the room. He laid down the book and stood as Chipman came inside. There was a rush of white vapor when winter struck the warm air of inside. The vapor disappeared instantly when the door closed.

"You're Tim Chipman?" the policeman asked.

"Yes."

"Constable Nevens. Fort McCrae."

They shook hands.

Nevens wasted no time in getting to the matter that brought him there. "You've run a railway from somewhere in the Granite Knob across the Lippel home claim, haven't you?"

"I've never heard of the Lippel home claim."

Nevens gave its location, and Tim recognized it to be the Randolph Cut, a block of white pine and Douglas that had been lumbered when he was a small boy.

"Yes, we crossed it."

"I'm sorry to cause you trouble, Chipman, but the claimant of that ground has objected to the line and enjoined you from using it. You'll have to settle it in court, or go around."

"We're a long way from court!" Tim barked.

"I'm sorry. There's no point in losing your temper with me. I merely enforce the law. Perhaps this is a piece of spite. But there's nothing I can do about it."

"Except stop my trains."

"Yes, stop your trains. Beginning tomorrow morning, as soon as I can post the boundaries."

"Can I see the paper?"

The Mounted Policeman showed it to him. It was signed by a Prince Albert magistrate, issued at the request of someone who called himself Frank P. Lippel.

"Who is he . . . Lippel?"

"The man who claimed that ground as a homesite fifteen years ago."

"Homesite! Stumps and rock. There was never a claim patented there. I saw an old cabin that someone had lived in back in the bush, but if you can find one acre of old cabbage patch . . ." There was no point in arguing. The policeman was merely doing his duty. "What can I do?" Tim asked.

"That's up to you. You can go down to Prince Albert and see the magistrate. Or maybe you can get hold of Lippel."

"Where is he . . . Lippel?"

"He crossed Chilkoos with me on the police sled."

"And got off at Brunner's headquarters down in Talka?"

Constable Nevens did not answer the question, but Tim knew he'd guessed it.

Nevens said: "He has stated his intention of moving up there while he waits for his wife."

"On the Randolph Cut?"

"On his claim."

Tim knew there was no legal claim to the ground, but the laws are always in favor of the legitimate home seeker, and that would be in Lippel's favor if he carried it to court. At any rate, Brunner would be able to tie it up for years.

He left the constable and went upcountry to the Chilkao Camp where he woke Ole Olsen. Olsen remembered that a claim had once been staked, but later abandoned, and after that the ownership had fallen to Chipman when the whole area north of

Chilkoos Lake had been classified as unsuited to agriculture. But despite that, all previous claims were still valid.

The constable was there at dawn to see that his road block was observed, and, when the sun glared on the snow at midday, Brunner men were chopping logs for a cabin.

Tim Chipman shouted to Nevens, asking him to bring Lippel around.

After a half hour wait, Constable Nevens brought a skinny, big-beaked man of fifty to the claim line.

"You're Lippel?" Tim asked.

"Yeah." Lippel answered because the policeman was there and he had to. His eyes had a weasel quality. By the look and smell of him he was just getting over a protracted drunk.

"When'd you take out this claim?"

Lippel named the exact date instantly. Brunner had seen to it that he'd memorized the facts.

"You know some of the old-timers here, don't you?"

"I don't remember anybody much. You timber men were tough on me. Never did me any favors. Why should I remember?"

"When were you born?"

"Don't think that's any of your business."

"I asked when you were born!"

He turned to the policeman. "I don't have to answer his questions, do I?"

"No. You're under no legal obligation to answer anything except things pertaining to this land."

"See?" Lippel laughed, showing a set of rotting teeth.

199

"How much will you take for a right-of-way across your ground?"

"It ain't for sale."

"That's what I thought." Tim made a gesture, showing he'd found out all he wanted from Lippel. He said to Nevens: "I don't want a spike of that railroad touched until this has been settled in court."

Nevens nodded. "It won't be."

Lippel whined: "This here's my farm and I ain't going to have . . ."

"If you touch that rail line, you'll be responsible for destroying Chipman property."

"It's a low-down dirty deal when somebody can shove a railroad through a man's property . . ."

Chipman could hear his whining voice for a hundred yards as the man waded snow back to his shanty.

The constable was there for two days. After he left, fifteen or twenty of Brunner's timber toughs camped on the ground, ready to stop any trespassing from the Chipman side.

Logs piled high at the railroad and the enthusiasm of the first weeks vanished. A couple of men quit. Tim Chipman hired an Indian dog driver and mushed across hills and lake ice to Prince Albert. Nothing he could do there, so he traveled on to Victoria, returning three weeks later with a report that he had a lawyer working. The lawyer hoped . . . But the weeks were stretching deep into February.

CHAPTER
SEVEN

Swiftwater Tilton was slightly drunk. Even after riding a railroad speeder through thirty-below cold from Vermilion, he was drunk. Drunk and in bad temper. Lynne was with him. He sent her away, and went inside the company house. The Chinese flunky had let the fire go down. He cursed, shouted: "Shen!" But Shen did not answer. He poured one from Brunner's bottle. After that there was nothing to do but build up the fire himself.

Swiftwater Tilton looked slack-faced, soft without being fat. His eyes were watery and pale. He'd once been one of the hardest travelers in the big timber, but one would never think that now. Whiskey and failure had ruined him. He strode the room a couple of times. Something was bothering him. He looked at the clock. Cold had stopped it. The degree of darkness outside indicated the time at about five o'clock.

Someone was outside, rapping at the door.

"Come in!" Tilton shouted in his whiskey-hoarse voice.

The door creaked open on cold hinges and a man shuffled as far as the arch, where he stood peering in.

It took Tilton a moment to realize the man was Frank Lippel.

"Well, Lippel, come on in. Have a drink."

The invitation surprised and pleased Frank Lippel. He'd been satisfying himself with moose milk, a combination of grain alcohol, water, and black strap molasses, so the bonded liquor looked good to him. He poured half a tumbler-full, glanced to make sure Brunner was not around, and drank it.

"You never been in this country before, Lippel," Swiftwater said. "What's your real name?"

"Lippel. My name's really Lippel."

Swiftwater spun without warning and smashed Lippel across the jaw with the back of his hand. It wasn't a hard blow, but it was so unexpected Lippel's head snapped to one side and he staggered backward, sprawling to the floor. He sat with his hands propped behind him, his dark, greasy hair strung over his eyes. He fingered it away in a baffled manner, and whined: "What'd you do that for?"

"What's your name?"

"Lippel, it's Lippel. Mister Brunner knows it's Lippel. He looked me up in Nelson. Said he'd been a month running me down. 'Are you Lippel?' he said . . ."

"You never been in this country before. I knew that the day you got here."

Lippel made it to his feet and circled, giving Swiftwater plenty of room.

"Anyhow, my name's Lippel."

"Where's the real Frank Lippel?"

"I don't know."

"Any relation?"

"Cousin."

"What if he shows up? He might, you know, if this thing appears in the legal advertising."

"He won't read no legal advertising. He's dead."

Lippel was edging toward the bottle. Suddenly he stopped. His eyes knifed to one of the inside doors. The door had swung a little, and firelight revealed a man. It was Brunner. He'd entered the rear door and had been standing there for some time.

Knowing he'd been seen, Brunner came on inside. He seemed a trifle preoccupied. "Glad to see you back," he said to Tilton. "Just saw Lynne. How was Prince Albert?" Then, to Lippel: "What do you want, Frank?"

"I come down to see if I could get some tobacco. And maybe a gallon. It's bad up there, them axe-handle stiffs you got shacked up with me been drinking every drop and ragging me to stop atop of it. When I came up here, you said . . ."

"I know what I said. Go over to the wanigan and get what you need." He saw Lippel looking at the bottle. "Pour yourself one, and get out."

When Lippel was gone, Brunner's gaze rested on Tilton. "I heard what you asked him. What do you have on your mind?"

It was evident they'd been having trouble even before Tilton and his daughter left for Prince Albert.

Tilton said in a raised voice: "I told you I wouldn't stand for that sort of business."

"Pull out then. Our agreement's only verbal. I intend to run Talka as I please."

"All right. I will get out."

His words surprised Brunner. He'd been letting the Swiftwater Timber Company exist at least nominally as an independent for more than two years, chiefly because of Lynne. His face, as he looked down at Tilton, was more than ever big-jawed and predatory. "You been outside, haven't you?" He meant Tilton had gone farther than Prince Albert. "Where you been . . . to Vancouver?"

"Yes."

"Who you been seeing down there?"

"Some old friends."

"Like Werheuser?"

"Yes."

"If you think I'll let you pull your timber reserves out of our combine and dump it in the lap of that outfit . . ." Brunner let it hang on that note. He looked huge and savage. In the past it had bothered him now and then that Tilton might try to sell his holdings elsewhere, but he'd always shrugged the thought off. During the last few months he'd heard rumors that the big Werheuser outfit was expanding its northern reserves especially in pulping spruce, and Tilton's visit had meshed too well. Brunner took a deep breath and managed to put a smile on his face. "Oh, now, Swifty, there's no point in us rowing. Think of Lynne. We . . ."

"I've been thinking of Lynne."

"Yes?"

"Have you ever told her the truth about that deal up there?" He meant the Lippel claim.

"Why should I? That's a business affair." The table separated them. Brunner circled the end of it. "But you did tell her. Is that it? You told her, and now you intend to sell out. To Werheuser."

"I haven't, but I will. Then I'm through with you."

Brunner's lips were drawn tightly across his teeth. He was fighting to hold onto his voice. "You've hated me all the time, haven't you? It was good old Croft to my face, because I was saving your haywire timber spread, but back in your mind you hated me. You wanted your chance. Now you think you can take your timber and Chipman's timber both away from my saws and break me. That's what you've been planning, isn't it?"

"I don't care whether I break you or not. I'm just sick of the crooked fight you're putting up."

"I'm like a wolf. I fight with the weapons I've got. That's what I've always done. Nobody ever gave it to me on a platter. I've fought for it every step of the way." He kept watching Tilton's face. He seemed to be smiling a little, grim and thoughtful. "Some things begin to make sense now, Swifty. That High Chilkao, for instance. I'm beginning to see how Chipman found out about the time limit when there were only two of us who knew about it. And that railroad business. I thought it was funny he'd change his plan about grabbing that train and make away with it just a half hour before we were ready to blast him out of the cab. You gave him the information, too, didn't you?"

205

Tilton didn't bother to answer. He turned, crossed the room, picked up his fur cap and overcoat. Brunner moved over to block his way.

"Where now?"

"I'm going to find Lynne. Then I'll see Chipman."

Brunner moved with the sudden, pouncing grace of a forest cat. He hesitated a second, poised on the balls of his feet. Then he set his heels, and his right fist came up with all the smashing strength of his big body.

Tilton tried to fend it off. A futile movement. The fist struck his jaw and snapped his head to one side like he'd struck the end of a hangman's rope. He was driven a dozen feet across the room. He crumpled with his head bent to one side, eyes open, but no sight in them.

Release of energy had only sharpened the savagery of Brunner's anger. He couldn't have stopped himself if he'd wanted to. He followed with long strides, grabbed Tilton by the front of his shirt, brought him to his wobbly legs, balanced him for a second, and hurled him across the room. Reflex kept the legs under him for five or six crumbling steps. Then he fell with his head against the stones of the fireplace.

He lay still. Brunner breathed deeply a few times. Anger as well as the effort had winded him. Silence of the room slowly asserted itself. Little sounds — logs snapping in the fire inside, from outside the *creak-creak* of someone walking on the snow-covered sidewalk.

Brunner noticed that Tilton hadn't moved. He walked over. Looked down on him. No breathing. None he could see. Brunner must have suspected that he was dead. For the moment he made no move to find out. He poured a drink, downed it slowly without taking his eyes off the man's slumped form. He put down the glass. Wiped his lips on the back of his hand. He looked around. No one could see through the frost-caked windowpanes. Shen, the Chinese, was down with lumbago. No one in the house.

Anger was all burned out of him now. His eyes were quick behind narrowed lids. He was about to lean over Tilton — stopped. More feet *creaked* on the walk. Suppertime. Men laughed. One footstep asserted itself, although it was quieter than the rest. Lynne Tilton. He recognized the rhythm of her walk even before her boots thumped the porch steps.

He was already through the archway, striding down the short hall. He jerked open the door.

"Lynne!" He drew up as though it was a surprise to find her there. "Lynne, I was just starting to look for you."

He was smiling. He went on out, closing the door after him.

"Where's Dad?" she asked.

"That's what I was going to ask you."

"Didn't he come to the house?"

"Yes, but something happened and he pulled out again. He'd been . . . well, you know how he was. He lit into my bottle while he was in there. Had a row with Lippel over some silly thing and stormed out saying he was headed for Chipman Camp. It's thirty below out, Lynne. He was in no shape for that."

"Why was he going to Chipman?"

"Oh . . . that Lippel fellow. Your dad was the one who brought him here. I understand Tim Chipman has been trying to prove his name wasn't Lippel at all. Claimed Swiftwater was a liar. That's how your dad got it. Now he's headed up there to settle it with Tim Chipman."

She was looking at him intently. "He wasn't angry with Tim when he rode up from Vermilion."

"He is now."

She started around him to open the door, but Brunner did not move. "There's been no fire all day. Colder than outside. You'd better have something to eat."

She could see smoke coming from the chimney. "Why don't you want me to go in?"

"I'd a little rather you didn't, Lynne, and for your sake I don't want to tell you why."

She stepped back, and he walked beside her, taking her arm. He was bareheaded and in shirt sleeves, but even so he didn't seem to mind the strong cold. They could hear Axe-Handle Ole's bellowing voice from the wanigan house as he rolled dice double or nothing for snoose. Brunner asked the girl to wait a moment, and jerked open the door.

"Ole!"

"Yah."

The big man put down the dice box and plodded out.

"Ole, there's something on the floor back in the big house. I want you to get it out without anybody knowing."

"What you mean . . . ?"

"Do what I said."

"Yah."

Ole stood in the door, looking grizzly-huge silhouetted against yellow lamplight, watching Brunner walk away along the snow-crusted corduroy.

Lynne Tilton stooped in the door of the house she shared with her father and old Kawe Oseechekun, their Cree housekeeper. She expected Brunner to leave her at the door, but he followed inside.

He smiled and said: "You act like you wanted to get rid of me. After all, I haven't seen you in three weeks . . ."

"It isn't that. It's just . . . well, I'm worried about Father. Don't you think we'd better send someone to bring him back?"

"All right." He still did not move. His hands reached and closed on her shoulders. "Lynne. Everything's the same between us, isn't it?"

"Why . . . yes. Why do you ask that?"

"I don't know. You've seemed . . . different. I still intend to marry you, Lynne."

She didn't answer.

"Did you hear me, Lynne?"

"Yes."

"Nothing's happened to make you change your mind? Nothing while you were outside . . . at Vancouver?"

"Nothing happened in Vancouver."

It seemed to be the answer he was waiting for. His hands were still on her shoulders. He drew her towards him, but she twisted and tried to free herself.

"Not . . . here. Kawe will be . . ."

"What of old Kawe? What difference does an Indian housekeeper make when two people plan to get married?"

"Please, Croft. Not now. I'm . . . tired. I'm worried."

He let her go. "I'll go out and look for him."

He went out, gave the door a hard jerk to close it. She looked at the unpainted panels for several seconds after he was gone. She seemed a little frightened. Old Kawe came in and asked whether Brunner or her father was coming for supper. Lynne didn't hear her. She went through the house, out the back way. She waded snow to her thighs in circling the house, cut through the camp to the railroad. Fresh footprints led along the grade as far as the train crew's shack, but not beyond. Swiftwater wouldn't be likely to take any other route to Chipman.

She stood for a couple of minutes, looking down across the camp. There was something wrong, and it made her sick. It wasn't like Brunner to stop her at the door. She remembered his words to Axe-Handle Ole. It always frightened her when Axe-Handle Ole was sent on some task.

She went back to the company house. Listened outside. Fire was yellowish against frosted windows. No lamp lighted. With her heart beating hard, she tried the door. It opened.

After a moment she called: "Croft!"

She was surprised by the loudness of her own voice. No answer. She stood in the arch. The room was growing warm. Flames from the fireplace rose and fell, and the table and chairs standing close to it sent big, blocky shadows shifting across walls and ceiling. She crossed the room. Her father's muskrat cap lay on the floor. She picked it up.

"Croft!" she cried.

There was no one in the house. She started toward the front door, stopped. Axe-Handle wouldn't go that way. Nor by the back door, either, for it was close to one of the bunkhouse sidewalks. There was a side door with its approaches hidden by sheds. She ran to it. The door opened easily. The marks of Ole's big boots were punched deeply in snow.

She followed the tracks for fifty yards and lost them amid a criss-cross of pathways between the bunkhouses and the mill. She was running now. It was a quarter mile to her house. She hurried upstairs, fumbled through darkness, and her hand touched the cold steel of a Winchester rifle.

She carried it down the stairs, stopped in lamplight, swung the lever down until she could see the glint of a brass cartridge. Old Kawe had appeared on her cat's paw moccasins and was watching with flat Indian lack of expression. She didn't say anything. Lynne went out, carrying the rifle over her arm.

Grub time at the mess house. She had a hunch Ole would not be there. Lamplight burned in the small bunkhouse where Brunner's more trusted employees occupied bunk stalls, which were the nearest thing any timber stiff ever had to a private room. She opened the door. The steamy smell of closed-in heat and old blankets struck her nostrils. A grease-dip lamp was burning, showing a small room with benches and a card-strewn table.

There was a passageway with the rooms leading from it. Someone was moving around. She walked on. Suddenly Axe-Handle Ole loomed before her. She'd pointed the gun instinctively and he drew up, huge, with his eyeballs staring.

"Stand where you are," she whispered.

"Yah."

He'd just finished making a balloon of the soogans on his bunk, and his war sack was in the middle of the floor half filled with clothing.

"Where are you going?"

"Aye . . . got yuh. Aye goin' to get outta har. Aye goin' quit."

"Why?"

"Aye goin' quit. Aye sick of workin' har."

"What's the matter?"

"This bane free country. Aye don' have to work har. Bane goin' down to Vermilion. Aye . . ."

He was frightened of the gun, but there was something else the matter.

"What did you find up there in the company house?"

"Nothin'. I didn't find a thing."

"Why did he send you there, then?"

"Aye don' know."

Her thumb brought the hammer back with a deadly *click*. She spoke through her small, white teeth. "There's only one way to treat liars."

"No. Don' shoot. Aye didn' do nothin'. Aye don' know nothin'. You let me get out har." Ole's face was loose from terror. Sweat glistened in droplets across his forehead. He looked like one stricken from ptomaine poisoning.

At that instant the door flew open, and Brunner spoke her name.

"Lynne! What's the matter with you?"

She whirled around, aiming the gun at him. Ole could have grabbed her from behind at that moment, but it didn't occur to him.

Brunner walked on and stopped with the gun muzzle almost touching his abdomen.

"Put it down, Lynne."

"Stay away from me!"

"What's got into you, anyway?"

"Where's my father?"

"I told you. I think he went to Chipman. He —"

"He didn't go to Chipman. He was inside the house. You did something to him so he wouldn't sell out, or tell Chipman about Frank Lippel."

"You don't really believe that about me, Lynne." His eyes traveled beyond her and rested on Axe-Handle Ole. "What did you tell her?"

"Aye didn' tell nothin'. Aye said . . ."

"Lynne! Ask Ole. Ask him if there was anything in the house. Your dad was drunk and strewed things around . . ."

"Didn' find nothin'," Ole said.

"You see, Lynne? You're suspecting me when you shouldn't. Put down the gun."

"Keep away!"

"You're not going to pull the trigger. You wouldn't kill me. There I'd be dead, and you'd have that hot gun in your hands. What good would it ever do you? All your life you'd know you were wrong."

The gun was still cocked, her finger clenched hard over the trigger. Brunner had a cold nerve. His hand closed on the barrel, and with a slow application of strength he turned it away. He could have taken it from her hands, but he didn't.

"You better go, Lynne. Go back to the house. Have Kawe fix you a hot toddy. You need one. I'll go out and see if I can find Swiftwater. I'll go all the way to Chipman if I have to."

He took hold of her shoulder. She'd been standing quite still, looking at him. Touch of his hand made her twist away and slide with her shoulders along the wall.

"Don't touch me!"

"You go to the house now, and think it over. You've been making a fool of yourself."

Excitement, and closeness of the room, made her feel dizzy. She restrained the impulse to run for the door. She backed away, felt behind her for the wooden latch, let herself outside.

Brunner watched until the door was closed. His face changed. He turned. Ole was watching him, took a step back. Brunner followed, and the big Swede kept retreating. The wall jolted his shoulders. He had his hands up.

"You let me get out of har," he whispered. "Aye bane quit this yob. Aye ain't goin' to be mixed up in no killin'."

214

"Why do you think I brought you here? Why do you think you draw double pay?"

"Bane rough Swede. Bane whip five, six men all alone. Bane fightin' man, yah. Ain't mixin' up wit' murder."

The word murder snapped Brunner's taut restraint. He swung his left hand, batting Ole's guard out of the way. He shifted his weight, and the right came like a sledge to the point of Ole's jaw. Ole's head slammed the wall. He was scared of Brunner, but he was cornered and he fought accordingly. He braced his feet and with shoulders still in the corner he swung his fists in massive arcs, battering his lighter antagonist, keeping him at a distance.

One of the blows struck Brunner and spun him halfway around. Instead of following it up, Ole tried to bolt for the door. Brunner tripped him. Ole sprawled face foremost, and Brunner was on him with his hobnailed logger boots. He came down with both feet, trampling Ole's head to the floor. It would have killed many men. Ole tried to push himself up. Brunner stepped back, measured the distance, booted him, did it again, again, each impact of his foot knocking droplets of mixed sweat and blood from the side of Ole's face.

In spite of it all, Ole got hold of a windowsill, forced himself to his feet. A right crushed his jaw and sent him down. He crawled on hands and knees toward the door.

"All right, get out." Brunner was filling his lungs. His knuckles were skinned and bleeding. He took a step, and the points of his hobnails left tiny prints of blood on the floor. "Get out. Don't ever let me see you again. Don't let anyone in this country ever see you again."

"Yah." Ole reeled to his feet. He stopped at the door, hand on the latch. "Yah. Aye go. Aye get out noo."

CHAPTER
EIGHT

Axe-Handle Ole reeled away from the bunkhouse without thought of direction until the frigid air of winter night brought him around. He sat down and rubbed snow over his face, cleaning it of blood. After ten or fifteen minutes he went back to the bunkhouse, opened the door, peered in. Brunner was gone. Others were still having supper. He went in, got his things, put on Mackinaw and Scotch cap.

He walked as far as the railroad grade. There he stopped before going down toward Vermilion Landing. His mind never worked rapidly, and he was still groggy from the beating, but certain things commenced to register. Brunner had killed Tilton. Only two persons knew about it — Brunner and himself. Brunner no longer trusted him. There was a good chance Brunner would call on the phone and leave instructions with Burgess down at Vermilion. Instructions to put him out of the way.

Ole was not used to doing his own thinking. Now on his own, a sick feeling of helplessness settled over him. Helplessness and fear. He stood until the cold commenced creeping through his logger boots, chilling his toes. At last he turned and started up the tracks toward Chipman.

The track ended at the torn-down barricade. He walked faster and faster, his gargantuan strides consuming distance until the windows of Chipman Camp gleamed through the forest fringe. He stopped. He knew there would be a sentry posted. He left the track and circled through the scrub undergrowth of a hillside, and thence to the camp along a gulch. He stopped in the shadow of some sheds. No one challenged him. Fifty paces away he could see the lighted windows of a bunkhouse. Men's voices inside. Rough. Scandinavian voices. In the background a concertina was whining. The concertina player found chords that suited him and commenced bearing down. It was a tune Ole had not heard since his old days in the States.

He moved close to the bunkhouse and stopped with one ear against the frosted window. His great, bruised face was slack and forlorn from lonesomeness. Men commenced singing. After a verse, Ole closed his eyes and weaved his huge body back and forth, humming the words with them.

> Aye bane workin' hard for you, Steena Stone,
> Aye bane workin' hard for you
> On Montana threshin' crew
> Yust bane workin' hard for you, Steena Stone!

Axe-Handle Ole was so intent he did not hear Ole Olsen coming until the old yard boss was right beside him. He whirled around and stood crouched, hands thrust out as though expecting an attack.

"Har, noo," Olsen said. "Who you bane, anyhow?"

"Bane Axe-Handle Ole." He kept his hands out and retreated a step or two, shaking his massive head. "Ain't causing no trooble. Bane lookin' for yob. Yah. Bane want yob from Chipman. Aye bane geude fightin' man. Geude faller, bucker, too. Yard man. River hog. Work hard, you let me stay har."

"Turn around," the elder Ole said. He kept Axe-Handle moving until the diffused light from the window struck his face. "Yimminy, who gave you those lumber-yack's measles?"

He was referring to the marks left by Brunner's hobs.

"Brunner. He beat hall out of me. Aye fall down and he yoomp on me."

"And then he fired you."

"Yah."

"Why'd he do that?"

Ole closed his mouth. His eyes were always small, and now, with the lids narrowed and his face swollen, they had almost disappeared. "You take me to Chipman. If he give me yob, Aye tell him why Aye get beat up."

Olsen looked around. He was wondering if it was some sort of a deadfall. The state of Axe-Handle's face indicated that it was on the level.

"All right. Aye will see if he's still up."

Tim Chipman had just come down from the Chilkao. There was no fire and he sat at the table in the big room, still wearing his sweater, Mackinaw, and wool cap.

He got up, surprised to see Axe-Handle Ole.

"Claims he wants a yob. Says he's got something to tell you."

"All right, Axe-Handle, what is it?"

"Bane tell it to you alone."

Tim nodded for Olsen to withdraw. He kept looking at Ole's face, fascinated by the terrific beating it was apparent he'd taken.

"Who gave you the measles? Brunner?"

"Yah."

"Why?"

"Aye try to quit. He beat hall out of me."

"Ever try to fight him back?"

Ole thrust out his two hands and slowly closed them. His fingers were the size of small bananas. They closed with difficulty, as each knuckle produced a popping sound. "Sometime Ole get him in these two hands. Sometime Ole . . ."

"Sure. But you're traveling in the wrong direction. Why'd you want to quit?"

"You give me yob? You . . ."

"I'll put you on bucking timber."

"OK. You my boss. Aye work for you."

"Now tell me about Brunner."

"Yah. Tonight he say, 'Ole, you go to house. Clean up mess.' Ain't swamper, but Aye go up there. You know what Aye find? Find dead man. You know who dead man is? Swiftwater Tilton. He bane beat up plenty."

Tim made no movement, but his face looked lean with shoe-leather brows beneath the reddish flame of the hanging lamp. "Brunner killed him?"

"Aye don' know. He yust coom to me, say, 'Ole . . .' "

"What did you do when you found him?"

"Carried him out behin' woodshed. Aye plenty scared, you bet. Don' want nothing to do with murder . . ."

"What was the row about?"

"Don' know nothin' . . ."

"Hadn't he just been to Prince Albert?"

"He yust get back. This afternoon. Lynne, too . . ."

"Where is she?"

"She at Talka."

"Does she know about her father?"

"She think plenty, Aye guess. She stick Winchester gun in my belly and say . . . 'Ole, you tall me about Swiftwater or I pull trigger.' But yust then in come Brunner. He tall her Swiftwater coom up har to Chipman. But that bane big lie . . ."

"She doesn't really know he's dead, then?"

"She guess plenty, though."

Tim Chipman picked up his Winchester, worked the lever once, and caught the cartridge as it spun out. He thoughtfully slid it back in the magazine.

"Ole, you know who killed my uncle . . . Clay Chipman?"

"Aye don' have nothin' to do wit' no killin' . . ."

"Who was it?"

221

"Somebody up har. Somebody Brunner have planted. Aye tank . . . Poole. Yah, Poole."

"Poole." Tim had always suspected Poole. "Is he down at camp?"

"Ain't seen Poole in two, three weeks."

Tim stepped outside. Ole Olsen was there, obviously still suspicious of Axe-Handle.

"We'll get some boys together. Don't push anybody. We may have trouble."

"Where you heading?"

"To Talka. I'll tell you about it on the way."

A slight breeze was blowing when Tim and eight men headed down the torn-up roadbed. The breeze felt soft, almost warm. A Chinook on its way, hinting an end to the long, dead cold of winter.

They'd traveled about half the distance when lanterns made points of light through spruce trees. Men were moving, repeatedly silhouetted against the light. Brunner's men — and Tim had a good idea why they were there, deep inside Chipman territory.

"Hey, up there!" a voice called.

Brunner's watchmen. Men withdrew beyond the fringe of lantern light. There were at least fifteen of them, so Brunner had him outnumbered by two to one.

Brunner's voice: "Chipman!"

"Yes."

Tim motioned for his men to stay back and covered the last fifty steps by himself. He could see a man walking up through the lantern light. Brunner. He spoke in a tight, hard voice. "Well, Tim, you have your gall, don't you?"

Brunner had a bolt action rifle over his arm. He stopped, with one of the lanterns strongly underlighting his face. Tim scarcely glanced at him. His eyes were on a blanket-covered form lying on an improvised spruce stretcher. The girl was standing just beyond.

"Lynne!"

"Hello, Tim."

"Your dad?"

"Yes."

"I'm sorry, Lynne." Brunner was walking up behind him. He turned and said: "It wasn't especially clever, bringing him up here, but I suppose it was the best you could think of under the circumstances."

Brunner's voice came with the tense whang of taut steel: "What are you trying to say?"

"I'm saying what everybody here already knows . . . that you rowed with him and lost your temper. You hit him too hard. He was inside the company house, and you sent Ole in to get him out. Ole left him by the woodshed and pulled out. So you had some of your other boys carry him here. Do you think anyone will believe that we did it?"

It jolted Brunner to have each turn called. He hesitated, eyes narrowed. "You're not talking to me. You're talking for Lynne. You're talking for the record. Everyone in our camp knows he started out to settle a score with you."

Tim didn't even seem to hear him. He was looking into Lynne's eyes. "I know you can't believe I ever had anything against your father, Lynne."

She'd been crying. She shook her head, showing she didn't want to answer. "Please! I don't know what to believe."

"Lynne . . ."

"Leave me alone."

Brunner listened and his hands clenched the rifle so hard his knuckles looked white and frozen. He'd taken a deep breath and was holding it. When she said she didn't know what to believe, he stepped forward, grabbed Tim by the shoulder, and flung him around. The force of it made Tim half fall. He caught himself and came to a crouch, instinctively leveling the Winchester.

"Don't fight," Lynne said in a tired voice.

Tim lowered the gun. He stood up. There was snow sticking to one leg where he'd fallen. "I'm sorry."

"Go away," she said. "Go away, all of you!"

Tim asked: "What are you going to do?"

"I don't know."

"You can't go back there." He gestured, indicating the Talka Camp. "Not now."

"Go away, please."

He moved back. It seemed impossible that she could believe Brunner's story. He was on the point of telling her about Axe-Handle Ole, but he checked himself. Brunner still wasn't sure where Ole was. He wouldn't hesitate to send a gang out to kill him.

224

Lynne looked around at the men, called a couple by name, and asked them to help with the stretcher. They lifted it, and without glancing back she followed her father's body down the track.

Brunner had placed himself in front of Tim. His lips were drawn tightly in a triumphant smile. "Don't try following her, Chipman. No jury in the North would convict me for killing you after what you've done tonight."

Tim turned without answering and went back to his men.

"You ain't letting her go . . . with him?" Riika said.

"She's got to make her own choice."

It was a silent group that followed Tim Chipman back to camp. He went to the big house and sat in his father's old place behind the plank table, staring across the room. He had no doubt Ole was telling the truth, but even if it got to court, the Swede's words wouldn't convict anybody. No one had seen Tilton get killed, or heard a quarrel.

He slept a few hours, and went outside. Dawn, and the Chinook wind was still blowing. He scooped up a handful of snow. It balled in his hand. The Chinook would blow itself out, and there would be other freezes, but spring was on its way. In three weeks more, the ice would be moving in the river.

He set out cross-country on snowshoes and reached the boundary of Lippel's claim. A short, broad-shouldered young man saw him and slouched that way.

"Got a light?" Tim asked.

The man walked to the boundary, rammed his rifle stock down in the wet snow, and fished a half dozen matches from his pocket.

Tim thanked him and offered his makings.

"I'm not man enough for that stuff," he said, referring to the strong Peerless. Then he asked: "Lookin' us over?"

"I was thinking of running a train through here." Tim said it as though it were a joke, and they both laughed.

"No, you wouldn't put any train through. Not for long, I'm thinking. Bullneck Brunner would be on that telegraph and have the redcoats up here in three days."

"Unless he had something to hide. Something about Lippel, for instance."

"Yeah?" The fellow was waiting for what Tim really had on his mind.

"I was thinking his name might be Smith."

He called Lippel a vile name. Then he added: "But his name's Lippel, all right."

"Even for a hundred dollars, his name's still Lippel?"

"Yeah. Even for a hundred. It wouldn't be any good to me in that pine box the *kiya tyee* would send me out of here in if I ever tried to whipsaw him."

He walked away and Tim shouted after him. "Think it over!"

"The hell with you."

CHAPTER
NINE

It was night when Tim got back to camp. He paused inside to look at the calendar, although he knew by the smell of the evergreen forest how close to spring it was.

Hob Miller shouted his name, and he stepped outside.

"Yes?"

Hob had taken over as watchman when Mahon went as straw boss on the Chilkao. A stranger was with him.

"Says he got a message for you, Tim."

"Here," the man said, handing over an envelope.

Tim opened it. It was not a message. It was a clipping from a newspaper. Too dark to read it. He carried it back to the house. An obituary notice. Frank Lippel. Frank Lippel had died six years before.

He crushed it in his hand without thinking. Then he understood it, put it away in the fireproof file.

"Who sent it?" he asked.

"Who'd you think?" the man growled.

He didn't want to mention Lynne's name.

"Any answer?"

"Just say thank you," Tim said.

The thought occurred to him that Swiftwater had learned about Frank Lippel while he was outside, and that the discovery had cost him his life.

Next morning the mail sled came in and the driver told him that Lynne was no longer at Talka. She'd gone back to the old Swiftwater Camp to bury her father. Now she had a dozen men at work around the old bolt mill, and it looked like the Swiftwater Camp was in business again.

That night he held a council of war at the Chilkao Camp. Thirty men were in the bunkhouse. They'd been there long enough to lay a blue layer of tobacco smoke across the room. It was hot, the door was open, and those sitting next to it could hear the wheeze of steam from the locomotive sitting at the jammer siding 200 yards down the slope.

"We're going through tonight," Tim Chipman said. "I'm not taking any of you to risk his neck for my timber. It wasn't part of your job when you hired out. So you can stay behind and nobody's going to think any the less of you for it, but if you want to come, you're welcome."

Nobody said anything for a moment. Finally Axe-Handle Ole got to his feet and stood hunched forward as though the ceiling were too low for him. "You wait har. All you faller wait har. Aye go up to that Lippel claim alone. Bane run 'em all out alone."

"There's some rough lads up there," Mahon said.

"Ain't many rough faller around when Ole get there. You wait one hour. Then you get 'long with engine. You

228

drive right through. Axe-Handle Ole knows what he's doing, by golly."

A Norwegian by the name of Jorgensen said: "Maybe you tank you whip them all alone, you dumb muscle-bound *Swenskapoika*."

"Yah, sure. One time in Nord Dakota bane whip one whole saloon full of Irishmen." Ole had recovered from his beating of the other night and was his old self again. He hooked thumbs in his suspenders and shouted: "You faller ever hear my song? Every lousy timber stiff in Wisconsin sing about Ole. You har?" Then he roared it out, stamping time with his hobnailed boots:

> My name it bane Yonson
> Aye come from Wisconsin,
> Aye working the hardwood stand,
> Aye ride to Shebaggin
> On Yim Hill's red wagon
> Wit' axe handle in my hand.
> Aye wear a red collar!
> Aye drank saxteen dollar!
> Wit' axe handle in my hand!

Still stamping his boots with a force that raised dust from the cracks of the rough plank floor, he seized his axe handle and marched outside.

"What you bane givin' him to drink?" Jorgensen asked.

"Swedes get that way on snoose," Mahon told him. "I've seen Swedes mix snoose and strong coffee into a drink that got 'em just as drunk as an Irishman gets on whiskey."

Tim glanced at his watch. He'd give Ole half an hour before starting out with the train. He knew there was a chance that Ole would double-cross him, but he couldn't hope to buck the engine through snow and ice without tipping off those Brunner men anyhow. He took three rifles from the storeroom and carried them to the engine cab. His men followed in groups of three and four. No one aside from Ole had actually volunteered, but apparently everyone planned to go. Some of them expected guns and complained when they weren't handed out.

"You didn't hire out here to get your heads shot off," Tim said.

Bob Marr answered: "Listen, if they start blastin' at me, I want something to answer 'em with."

"Sorry, boys, but I'm not going to turn this into a war. Not right now."

He was fairly certain that Brunner had not given his men orders to shoot. Merciless fighter though he was, he wouldn't want to kill a man blocking ground to which he had no legitimate claim. Tim had little doubt it would end in shooting before the big drive, but that would be Brunner's last resort. Marr kept grumbling, and he suspected that some of the others had revolvers thrust under their Mackinaws, but he couldn't be sure.

The half hour had gone by when the train was ready, so they started out, pulling a full load of timber, plowing frozen snow. It was hard going. Each fifty or seventy-five yards the engine was forced to stop, back up, plunge forward again, and at times the entire crew was out ahead with shovels clearing the track.

Timber stood in solid walls on each side for several miles, then the track emerged into the brush and stumps of a logged-over area. The Lippel claim was slightly more than one mile away, and Tim noticed a glow above the tips of second-growth spruce that seemed to mark its position. The glow became steadily brighter, silhouetting the spruces, black against red.

"Now what's that?" Mahon muttered. Keeping the Winchester under his arm, he climbed to the tender where he had a better view. Tim heard him chuckle and whack the leg of his tin pants. "Why that tricky Swede! So that's what he drew the coal oil for!"

"Coal oil?"

"Sure. A two-gallon can of coal oil. I saw him getting it at the storehouse before dark."

The glow built up higher and higher. It underlighted a billow of smoke, and against the smoke were clusters of ascending sparks. A gun exploded with a high-pitched whang and rattled away in echoes. Just the one shot.

Mahon said: "Well, Axe-Handle, you died in a good cause."

Ole Olsen, the third man in the cab, spoke: "Aye wouldn't be too sure one bullet kill that big Swede."

The engine had been running without obstruction for almost 300 yards. A drift stopped it. Three or four minutes were consumed in bucking through. By that time the fire had passed its apex and was rapidly diminishing. It was always like that when a cabin burned — a roar of flame as the roof was consumed, then a day or two while fire slowly groped its way through the thick log walls.

Tim cut the headlight. Easier to watch the surrounding country without it. There was no moon, and the stars were graying off toward dawn. A glow, like phosphorescence, rose from the wide sweep of snow.

Mahon was still on the tender, crouched, his Winchester ready. Tim and Ole Olsen leaned from the windows. No sign of movement. They were at the Lippel claim. The engine eased up to the length of board that the mounted policeman had nailed between two trees to form his legal barricade. The board bent and splintered. Tim kept the engine barely on the move for fear a rail had been loosened or removed as an extra precaution against passage.

The cabin came in sight — or what had been the cabin. Nothing left now except a heap of glowing logs with the rock chimney towering above. Movement became visible. Two men. They were walking toward them.

"Hey, you there!" Mahon called.

"Bane Axe-Handle Ole!"

Olsen said: "Aye tell you one bullet don't kill that Swede."

Ole was half leading, half dragging the other man: Lippel.

Ole stopped knee deep in snow by the engine steps. He was holding Lippel by the back of his Mackinaw; he thrust him at arm's length. Lippel's bruised lips indicated that Ole had done some convincing.

Ole shook him and said: "You stand up, noo!"

Lippel tried, but his knees bent and he'd have fallen beneath the engine if Ole hadn't kept holding him. Ole cursed, jerked him upright, snapped him back and forth. "You har me? You stand up noo!"

Lippel's cap fell from his head and his greasy dark hair strung across his face.

Tim said: "That's enough, Ole."

"Yah."

Ole gave up trying to get Lippel to stand. He got a good grip and lifted him high overhead, held him for a second or two with one hand, and dumped him face foremost in the engine cab.

Frank Lippel got to hands and knees. No injury had kept his legs from functioning. It had been fright.

"Keep him away," Lippel whispered. "Keep that Swede away from me. He tried to kill me. He tried . . ."

"How do you know that *I* won't kill you?" Tim asked.

"No. Not you. You wouldn't . . ."

"How do you know I won't haul you outside and dump you in that Mountie's lap? You lied to him and signed your name to it when you said you were Frank Lippel."

"I didn't do nothing. It was Brunner. He hunted me out in Nelson and said as long as Frank Lippel was my cousin and me being his heir . . . Listen, Chipman, I'll get out of the country and never come back. I'll sign a paper telling I ain't Lippel. I'll sell you the claim."

Glow from the firebox door cast a reddish sidelight on Lippel's face. It was repulsive from fear.

"Where are your boys?" Tim asked, jerking his head at the burned cabin.

"They ran out. Yellow cowards, run out and left me there with that Swede. They didn't have the guts to fight him, all ten of them put together."

"Are they armed?"

"You mean have they got guns? Couple, three. Poole, maybe. Most of the guns got burnt up in the shack. I had forty dollars in —"

"Poole? He was there?"

"Yah. He was there. Been there for two weeks."

Tim's hand closed hard around the Winchester. He looked beyond Lippel, across the winter night. "Which way'd he go?"

"I don't know which way anybody went. Shagged out to the Talka Camp, I suppose."

"You can't find him tonight," Mahon said. "We'll run that Poole down. Listen, Tim . . . you're not sure Ole was telling the truth about him killing Clay anyhow."

"Bane tellin' true!" Ole bellowed.

"Sure, Ole," Tim said. "You've been telling the truth."

They had little trouble getting the engine the remaining distance across the Lippel claim, or on to Mad River.

On succeeding days, work increased in tempo. Only a few men were still falling and bucking timber, but three shifts loaded logs with the jammer at Chilkao siding, hauled to Mad River, swung logs over the deep cañon with high tackle and stacked them on the ice below.

Spring was coming. Each day the snow turned soft and wet so it stuck to a man's boots, then froze to a hard glaze after nightfall. The south ridges were bare, and streams tunneled beneath deep layers of snow in the narrow gulches. Soon it became apparent that less than two-thirds of the cut would ever reach river ice before the breakup. There was no time or means to bring more tackle from Prince Albert.

One morning a team of horses came in sight pulling a sled loaded with pulley and wire rope. Lynne had sent it from her Swiftwater Camp.

"I'll be back with another load tomorrow," the man said, "and I hope your boys keep their mouths shut about where you got it."

The next day passed, but the man did not return. Tim Chipman rolled up in a blanket and tried to sleep in the shelter of some yarded logs, but he gave up after midnight, got up, and trailed the sled down to Lynne's Swiftwater Camp. It was mid-morning when he sighted it standing on one of the arms of Chilkoos Lake.

The bolt mill was a heap of smoldering beams and blackened sheet metal. Two men stood in the door of a shanty watching him walk that way.

"What happened?" he asked.

"Burned," the younger of the two answered.

"Who did it?"

"I don't know anybody did it. It just burned."

"Where's Lynne?"

"Went yonder to look for Chipman."

"I'm Chipman."

"You? She said she was headin' for your Cañon Camp."

"When?"

"Early this morning."

He went back, thinking perhaps he'd missed her somewhere along the way, then he headed across a hogback ridge and dropped through timber at Talka. No one paid any special attention as he walked across the tracks and down on the company buildings. A man came from the wanigan and shaded his eyes against spring sun glare to see who he was.

"Chipman?"

It was Burgess, the storekeeper from Vermilion.

"Hello, Cade. Where's Brunner?"

"He ain't here."

"I asked where he was."

Burgess retreated a step, his face truculent. "I don't know."

"What's he done with Lynne Tilton?"

"Him done with her! What kind of notion you got, anyhow? He ain't done nothing with her. She headed outside this morning."

"Outside to Prince Albert? How?" The season was late for sled passage across Chilkoos Lake, and to reach Prince Albert would necessitate a 100-mile trip around the high edges of Chilkoos and Nokewin. "You're lying, Burgess."

"Don't call me a —"

Tim started forward to seize him by the collar like he had the day of his arrival at Vermilion the fall before, but Burgess was wary of him this time and already he

236

was sliding along with his shoulders to the building. Three men were watching from the wanigan's open door.

"Keep your hands off me!" Burgess shouted. An axe was leaning against a windowsill. Burgess grabbed it, hurled it with sudden overhand strength. Tim bent, letting it cut the air over his back. It gave Burgess his chance to reach the end of the porch. There he turned. He spoke while still backing off. "Get out o' here, Chipman, or I'll get a Winchester and blast you."

Tim Chipman looked at the men in the door. "Where's Brunner?"

A mill hand said: "He ain't been here all day, far as I know."

"How about Lynne Tilton?"

"Ain't seen her in two weeks."

Burgess was running along a corduroy toward the bunkhouses. He'd be looking for help.

Tim walked through the company house. No one there. It looked as though neither Brunner nor the girl was in camp.

CHAPTER
TEN

He cut past the mill, crossed the log boom, and headed north along the river, reaching Chipman Camp an hour past nightfall. He slept there — his first night in a bed for more than a week. Worry for Lynne kept gnawing at his mind. He had no doubt Brunner had burned her out because she'd sent supplies to Cañon Camp.

He rode a loaded log car down grade to the cañon and climbed the spar tree for a look below. The cañon was not an abrupt drop. It was cracked and columnar, like all weathered basalt, a series of pillars and sheer walls ending on rough ice that had frozen over the rapids. Actually little of the ice was visible, so deeply was it covered with logs. Logs end to end, pointing downstream. Water flowed here and there, breaking from beneath. At one spot seven or eight logs were upended, like the miniature start of a jam.

"Ice startin' to move," Ole Olsen said.

"Already?"

"Yah. Plenty snow this year. She'll get goin' good about tomorrow."

That evening a Beaver Indian came from the back country pulling a toboggan loaded with pelts. He reported the upper Mad full of float ice that had dammed the stream, forming a three-mile stretch of lake.

All night the camp was up, listening to the distant boom of ice, expecting any instant that the dam would give way with a flood to start the great drive. Ole Olsen was tired and brittle-tempered. "We better go upriver and blast. One time, ten yar ago, Aye see whole crest fade away behind ice dam."

"We'll wait a day."

"Visitor, Tim!" Jorgensen shouted.

It was Lynne Tilton. She hurried towards him. She was dressed like a man in blanket-lined trousers, boots, a Mackinaw, and red plaid cap, but despite her rough clothes she seemed more beautiful than ever. She stopped with her hands reaching and touching his shoulders. She was out of breath.

"Tim! I hope I'm in time."

He was too relieved at seeing her to realize what she'd said.

"What?"

"Brunner. His men are coming up here."

"To attack us?"

"No. To blast the cañon wall. He could jam your log drive. He's been hauling dynamite all yesterday afternoon. All night. Tons of it. I couldn't get away. I was at Vermilion and I knew what they were about, but . . ."

"He was holding you prisoner!"

"It was nothing. He found out about the equipment I'd sent you and swore to stop me. He had old Kawe watching me, but I got away. Listen to me, Tim. You'll have to stop him. He'll put rock into the narrows and block every log you have. You never will get them out. You'll have to hurry. Before dawn."

"Sure." He shook his head as though awakening. "You say it's at the narrows?"

"I'm not sure. I think so."

The narrows were a mile downstream.

Jorgensen was listening. Without waiting instructions he started down the trail, but Tim shouted, making him stop: "Not alone! Brunner means business."

Jorgensen came back.

"Go find Olsen. Mahon, too. Axe-Handle, if he wants to come. Tell them to bring some more of the boys. Marr, and the others who have been spoiling for the smell of gunpowder."

She said: "He'll be ready for trouble."

"I know. I won't let the boys walk into any ambush."

Word of it raced through the camp. The tackle came to a stop, with logs dangling in mid-air high above the cañon ice.

"Keep moving!" Chipman shouted. "Swing those logs! We'll take care of Brunner."

Axe-Handle Ole came up looking truculent and unwilling.

"What's wrong?" Mahon asked. "Losin' your nerve, Ole?"

"Ain't losin' no nerve. Bane fightin' man. But don't fight wit' guns. Bane whip whole saloon full of Irishmen wit' axe handle, but guns . . ."

"Lay off him," Chipman said. "I'm not asking any man here to duck bullet lead if he doesn't want to."

240

There were more men willing to go than there were guns to supply them. Nine men started out, headed by Tim Chipman. They were scarcely fifty paces below the spar tree when a rifle whanged with a high-velocity sound, and a bullet whipped hard through the spruce branches overhead. The rifle was about 300 yards away, judging by its report. Men scattered, finding cover in timber.

Machi, the timber topper, was out ahead. He came to the edge of a small clearing and started to cross. The rifle crashed again, and this time its bullet dug a long, black furrow, mixing earth with the wet snow less than four feet to his left.

"Get back!" Tim shouted, but Machi weaved forward, running at a low crouch. A third bullet ripped close. He plunged headlong, lay on elbows behind a deadfall.

Gunsmoke drifted from a spot on the logged-off hillside ahead. The first rays of morning sun caught it, and Chipman knew the man was holed up behind a fallen log. He waited with his Winchester leveled, glimpsed movement, touched the trigger. His bullet struck the log close to its top surface. It scattered thick, blackish bark and left a foot-long scar. Machi was crawling again.

"Get down!"

Another rifle. The bullet hit Machi and spun him halfway around. He dropped the rifle, fell. He crawled on hands and knees, only half conscious from bullet shock.

Tim said to the others: "Circle. Keep to the timber, and don't take any chances you don't have to. Mahon, you're in command. Try to make that hillside. It overlooks the cañon. I'm going down for Machi."

He found cover behind a stump, moved carefully, concealed himself behind dead slash, then in a low growth of leafless buck brush, and reached mid-clearing without drawing a shot. He could go no farther without exposing himself to the gun up the hillside, so he crouched and ran, weaving, trying to make a poor target. He was almost to Machi before a gun sounded. Then there were two reports, one close to the other. A bullet passed so close it popped the air by one ear.

He dived face foremost and dragged himself from elbow to elbow through moss and wet snow, at last coming to a crouch by Machi. The Finlander was shaking off bullet shock, trying to get his shirt unbuttoned.

"Hold it." Tim drew a Bowie and slit the fabric. The bullet had taken him in the side, had shattered a couple of the lower ribs, and gone on again. "You're not hurt bad."

"Sure, no. Take more'n this to flatten me. Got chew snoose?"

"Peerless do?"

"Yah."

Machi took a three-finger grab from Tim's package and thrust it in one cheek. He grinned then from a lopsided face. "You patch me up, Tim, and give me that old Four-Oh-Five Winchester again. I been waitin' to get my shots at Brunner all year."

242

Tim tore a handkerchief in half, folded it, making two pads, and bound one to each of the bullet openings with strips torn from his own shirt. He said: "You stay here till the boys clean out a couple of ambush guns, then I'll get you back to camp."

"You give me my gun and leave me alone. I'll get back to camp when I please."

Tim had long known the futility of reasoning with a Finlander where battle was involved. There's an old saying that a Finlander will fight for three days after he's dead. It was only a slight understatement.

"All right. There's your cannon."

Tim handed him his rifle and went on, by himself. He stopped after covering forty or fifty yards. Scrub timber was thick, shutting him in on all sides. There was a low hill at one side, and the cañon at the other.

A man was running. He could feel rather than hear the heavy thud of his footsteps. A gun exploded, leaving a rattle of echo from the cañon walls. It became quiet. It was so quiet he could hear the screech of steel brake shoes as a loaded car of logs came to a stop after coasting down the long grade from Chilkao.

Men were talking. Voices out in the bush. Unfamiliar voices, filled with tension. Someone shouted: "Monk . . . git yourself out o' there. You hear me, Monk?" He knew then they weren't setting powder at the narrows, but here, close at hand, in the rapids. They were spitting fuses, and one of the men was slow in getting out.

"I'm all right," a voice said.

He waited. For a quarter minute everything was dead still. Then the explosion hit. It wasn't loud. It was a reverberation like thunder, and the earth jolted beneath him. A rush of air sang through spruce branches. A rock large as an anvil flew high and descended with a crash in timber. Then there was a long, diminishing roar as the cañon wall crumpled and spilled itself across ice, water, and logs below.

Men were shouting. Strange voices — the voices of Brunner's men. Those timber toughs he'd been importing all winter from Prince Albert and beyond. Tim knew by the excellent tone that the blast had been successful. He started back and met Machi.

"We can't do anything about it now."

"No? Well, I got some blasting to do!"

Tim Chipman let him go. He ran back to camp. The remainder of his crew were dashing around, arming themselves with axes, and one of Olsen's Swedes carried an improvised bomb — four sticks of dynamite crammed in a baking powder can, with a full inch of fuse.

He told them to take it easy, walked to the spur tree, hooked a set of spurs to his boots, and got ready to climb. Lynne ran up beside him. She was holding a long-barreled .32 Colt revolver in one hand.

"Don't shoot." He grinned.

"They'll pick you off up there, Tim . . ."

"I die hard."

Tim passed his belt rope around the tree and made the snap fast to his waist. He'd been up many trees in a topper's rôle, and he climbed swiftly, sinking the steel gaffs and repeatedly tossing the belt upward ahead of him. Someone saw him and fired. The bullet sank in heartwood, sending a little tremble along the big tree. He kept going. The gun was at least 400 yards away, and he had the tree itself for protection. He stopped near the high, swaying top and leaned back, supported by spikes and rope to look in the depths of the cañon.

Dust was drifting up, a faint, reddish haze. The charge had been placed to shatter one of the basaltic pillars and spill it across the cañon. It looked like a little thing, viewed from above, but he knew it was obstruction enough to cause a log jam that might easily hold during the scant four or five days of floodwater that alone could float his big logs down the Mad. From his high position he could hear the deep groan of ice and wood. Logs had to float down the straight width of the cañon and were already piling up where the channel was pinched against the far wall. They'd jam, but there was a chance that the full strength of spring flood would end by carrying the mass before it.

He descended. Men watched his expression to tell how bad things were. He saw Olsen and said: "Ole, get the engine and bring those twenty cases of dynamite from the home camp. I think there are half a dozen at Chilkao, too. Get it all down here."

It was mid-afternoon when the engine returned, hauling its cargo of powder. By then the river was rising rapidly, its surface an amorphous mass of logs and flotage. A man sent upriver to check on the ice dam came back with word that it had disintegrated.

There was a minor crest at sundown. Then the river dropped until midnight when it started rising again, steadily. The spring breakup was on them.

Water kept rising all through the next day, and that night. Logs piled higher, rolling in a huge, tangled heap above the rockslide. Sometimes, with a booming sound, the jam would move, threatening to collapse forward with each new rise of the water.

Olsen came up from the river, cold and wet after an hour spent measuring the water. "Ain't goin' any higher. Maybe this crest'll hold one, two days."

Tim nodded grimly. It was the word he was waiting for. "We can use that dynamite now."

"Yah, sure."

"You've seen lots of log jams, Ole. Can we open it?"

"Wit' twenty-six cases dynamite? Yah, sure. Wit' twenty-six cases powder, we blow half those logs clear to Beaver Lake, by golly."

When Tim asked for volunteers to carry dynamite, every man in camp lined up. There was a good switchback trail leading to the bottom, but, in spite of that, moving dynamite to the jam would be a tough and dangerous job.

Men lined up while Steve Riika made rope slings with arm loops and tumplines. Tim shouldered the first case and started for the cañon.

The trail wound through scrub timber, down a steep gully, and swung out to follow a ledge along an eighty-degree cliff. It was an ancient portage trail that had been traveled by *voyageurs* for 100 years before the arrival of timber men. Projecting, wire-tough roots of

246

juniper shrubs gave occasional hand holds. A bullet struck, making a high, metallic screech as it glanced from the cliff. Hard rock pellets stung his face, temporarily blinding him. He started to flatten himself against the wall and realized he'd merely push the case of dynamite out for a target — an invitation to be blasted to atoms. He backed away, in partial protection as a second slug struck and glanced, leaving a bluish streak on the rock about two feet over his head.

He went back to the gulch. His face was bleeding from rock fragments that had struck it. "We'll have to wait," he said.

Machi was there. His wound prevented him from carrying powder, but there was a rifle over his arm. "Don't wait! We'll go down there and clean 'em out."

"Brunner has more men than we do. They're ambushed. We wouldn't have a chance."

"Then what . . . ?"

"We'll have to wait for night. And pray it's a dark one."

Hours dragged slowly. Men waited, silent and apprehensive, listening to the steady roar and grind of the log jam.

With twilight came a slight, spring mist, drifting downstream on a breeze from the north. Stars came out during twilight, and there would be an early moon.

Tim Chipman stood up and got the fifty-pound case of dynamite once again on his back. Others did the same and lined up behind him. Few words were spoken. They followed in single file as he walked past the first path and started down a second, more tortuous route toward the bottom. It was not switchbacked like the first. Scarcely a trail at all. A mere series of hand- and footholds leading down the deeply creviced side. His foot dislodged a stone that rolled crashing below. The sound could scarcely have been heard over the roar of the river, but at the next instant a gun knifed the black shadow of timber on the far rim. The high-velocity slug struck twenty feet wide and started a rattling stream of rocks toward the bottom.

The gun flashed again, and this time there was an answer from Machi. It started a hammering volley from both sides of the cañon wall. Blind shooting. Those timber toughs of Brunner's had been posted there all day, and now they were itching to burn powder.

None of the bullets came close, but Tim Chipman realized the impossibility of moving farther, even at night, down the cañon side. He clambered back up the cliff and cursed for a while. By himself, a man might reach bottom without trouble, but with those boxes of powder . . .

His men were gathered in a silent group along the rim. Occasionally a bullet would whip through, clipping the twigs of spruce trees. Tim got the powder off his back and said: "Let's get this stuff under cover before a stray bullet nicks it."

He walked on, up a slight rise of ground. He noticed that Lynne had come from somewhere and was at his side. She said: "Tim. There must be something . . ."

"Sure there is." He stood for a while, feeling the north breeze against his face. "If that breeze holds, and if the flood holds." He glanced at her. "A man needs a little luck on his side when he goes up against someone like Brunner."

"What do you mean about the breeze holding?"

"There's a downdraft through the cañon. A few slash fires might give us a chance."

Building smudge heaps took a couple of hours, and, after they were lighted, more time elapsed before thick billows of smoke were rolling through the cañon.

Northern nights were short at that season. Dawn came with sun reddish-brown through smoke. Sometimes an air current would eddy through, blowing a hole in the solid grayness, giving a view from wall to wall, but the glimpse would be brief.

"We'd better get some rifles spotted down there first," Tim said. "Can you travel?" he asked Machi.

"Never ask a Finlander can he travel!"

"All right, come along. You too, Mahon. And Jorgensen. The four of us will be enough. Riika, you can lead off with the powder. Get out your watch. Wait ten minutes. If I don't warn you, come along. But take it slow. I don't want anybody falling fifty or a hundred feet with a case of powder on his back."

"Not on me, anyhow," Mahon muttered.

Chipman jerked his head and said: "All right!" He led his riflemen into the cañon.

After forty feet, the broken rim rocks dissolved in gray, smoky uncertainty. No view of the far wall, or of the river below. They circled the cliff where Tim had been driven back by bullets the day before, found a switchback, and felt the cold breath of the river rising to meet them. Less smoke down there. A slight movement of air continually followed the river as though pulled along by the current's vacuum.

"Easy!" Tim said, looking at the uncertain footing of the jam and the depths to which a man might fall. "No getting a man out if he fell in there."

They followed the cañon side for another fifty feet, and found an upcast bridge log that took them to the main segment of the jam. It was difficult walking. Logs lay in every conceivable angle; many were slick from water and ice. Between them, everywhere, one could look down twenty or thirty feet and see the river beating itself into a racing froth.

They moved slowly, testing each step for footing. Most of the logs were solidly locked, yet the mass itself continually swelled and contracted like some monster breathing. Mahon said something, but his words were drowned by the roar of the water. Logs commenced to heap up, finally forming an overthrust that looked downriver. It took five minutes of hunting to locate the key mass.

Tim pointed to it, shouted in Mahon's ear as he came up: "There's your main charge! We'll put ten cases in there! That should break it loose, all right, but we'll set a couple of cases against each shore, too, just to break the drag!"

Mahon had a peavey in his hand. He set it against each of several logs, trying them, testing them for feel. The key log, if there was one, would be deeply buried. Still, it would be fun to hunt for it.

Tim Chipman knew what was on his mind and his teeth shone in a smile. "What'd you do if you did find it? Would you jerk it free and ride these downriver?"

"What?" Mahon shouted.

Tim shook his head, meaning it wasn't important.

A vagrant wind eddy blew a hole in the smoke, and they could see high up the cañon walls, but after a couple or three seconds, the hole closed again. Jorgensen was saying something about not caring to be caught there with half a ton of powder if wind came to blow the smoke away. The roar of water covered half his words.

Mahon pointed, and they could dimly see Riika balancing as he walked the slanting bridge log with a case of dynamite roped to his back. A gun whanged, its concussion unusually sharp, held in by the cañon walls. The bullet struck with a dead sound, carving wet chips from a log near the crest of the jam over Mahon's head. Powder flash briefly pinpointed the gun's position high on the side.

Tim Chipman was facing that way. He tossed up his Winchester and fired, all in one movement. It was a snap shot, but it caught the man as he moved to new cover along the wall. He was hit. He sprawled over, caught himself, still had enough strength to get around the edge of a steep gully. From there the wounded man fired again, again, without aiming, the bullets whining off, raising quickly repeated claps of echo.

"More of 'em," Mahon said.

Their movement was uncertain through smoke. Jorgensen and Machi found cover among upended logs and commenced whanging away. Little to aim at, but the bullets seemed to be forcing Brunner's men higher up the wall. Riika, despite his years and burden, trotted across with a swift balance derived from a lifetime of log driving. He lowered the case of powder, helped Tim slide it in a natural cavern deep beneath the logs.

"Caps?" Tim asked.

"Ole has 'em."

Other men came, unloading dynamite. Riika and Tim kept lowering it. Ole Olsen tore a slat from one case, drew out a stick of explosive, and primed it with a Number Eight cap. Tim himself measured and cut the fuse at seven feet. The way most of that fuse burned, seven feet would give a man three and a half minutes.

"Cutting it a little close?" Mahon shouted.

Tim shrugged his shoulders. He'd been tempted to cut the fuse a lot shorter. He left it unlighted, located the drag points along shore, and placed two cases of powder at each of them. In all, the operation had consumed less than twenty minutes. Wind was stronger now, and wide rifts were being blown in the smoke.

"Get out, boys!"

His voice was eaten up by the roar of water. He walked among the men and got them on the move. Machi and Jorgensen were still shooting.

He shouted to Jorgensen: "You spit that shore fuse! I'll get the other two! We'll have to move fast!"

He'd cut Jorgensen's fuse at nine feet. That would give him three-fourths of a minute to get closer. Then he could spit the main charge and still have it to go first. The other drag shot was cut at five feet. If things went right, all should be detonated within ten or fifteen seconds of one another.

He hunkered with his Winchester across his knees and watched Jorgensen get the fuse lighted. He failed with the first match. At last he got it going, sprang to his feet, and started across the jam with long, loping strides.

Tim Chipman counted slowly, measuring the seconds. At twenty-five, Jorgensen was out of sight against the far wall. He had a match ready at thirty-five, lighted it at fifty. The fuse was notched. It ignited and hissed burning powder. He glimpsed movement, glanced around. The wall was an uncertain, milky blue through drifting smoke. He could see nothing. He stood, counting, and the movement was there again. This time he knew what it was. A rope had been lowered from above and was slowly swinging back and forth.

Brunner's voice, sudden, snarling, from the smoky wall above: "Get down that wall." He was speaking to one of his men. "Get moving, or I'll put a bullet through you!"

A man slid into sight. He saw Tim and dropped. He hit the steeply slanting wall of the cañon and an instant later was out of sight beyond the heaped logs. Despite smoke and his rapid descent, Tim realized that the man was Dick Poole.

Poole remained out of sight and Tim moved back, balancing from log to log, his gun ready. He glimpsed the black, curling length of fuse, crouched, laid down his gun, scratched a match.

Poole came up and fired, the bullet whipping so close its air stream extinguished the match. Tim let himself fall face foremost to cover, taking the rifle as he went. He was down, among logs, feet almost in water. Poole, glimpsing him, thought his bullet had cut him down. He stood, took three balancing steps, and saw Tim rising with the Winchester. It was a sharp, close-spaced exchange. Two shots that a single second would have covered.

Poole was hit. He fell, struck belly down across a log, and slid out of sight. Gunfire had created a moment's diversion. A second man, seizing the chance, swung down on the rope and dropped to the log jam thirty feet from the wall. The man landed on his feet and momentarily remained delicately balanced with his hobs set in one of the high-slanting logs, rifle held overhead. Brunner!

Brunner sprang to another log, and hurled himself forward, out of sight. Tim was shifting position, expecting a bullet from Brunner's gun. It did not come. Brunner was headed across for that key charge to jerk the fuse.

Tim didn't dare go directly forward to intercept him. It would be suicide. Instead, he climbed over the jam's downstream bulge and moved along clinging to log butts, his hobnailed boots hunting precarious footing.

One of the logs gave way, twisted an inch or two. A little thing, but enough to make some of the bark slough off, and his corks slip. He fell, caught himself on hand and elbow, waist deep in gushing water. His rifle clattered once and disappeared in the crazy cribwork of logs.

He pulled himself up, blanket-lined trousers heavy and cold on his legs. They made it hard going. Things looked different here, with the jam towering steeply above. He guessed his position, pulled himself to a crouch. Brunner was standing directly beneath him.

The fuse had burned out of sight and the man was going to one knee to reach for it. He saw Tim Chipman at the final instant. He fell back, seized the rifle, and tried to bring the barrel around like a club. Tim was springing, forearm up for protection. The rifle glanced. They collided. Tim's weight carried Brunner back among the tangle of logs.

For a second it seemed that he was wedged there. Tim found footing, pulled himself to one knee, but Brunner had hold of his shirt. Tim tried to fight loose. He drove a left. It mashed Brunner's lips. He spit blood, cursed through his teeth. He'd got his balance. He let go of Tim's shirt and started what looked like a left-hand punch. At the final instant he let the punch go short, bent his arm sharply, and drove his elbow to Tim's jaw.

It had the sudden, abrupt impact of a club. Tim's ears were ringing. He didn't retreat. He braced himself and tried to force Brunner back. Brunner had the better footing now. He smashed up with the one-two left and right — the same blows that had put Ole on the ground back at Talka Camp. Tim felt himself going. He tried for new footing, a blind, instinctive move. The corks of his left boot slipped. He fell, striking his back across the log.

He realized Brunner's boots were coming. He tried to twist aside. He slipped between the logs. His legs dangled. Beneath was river. He clung, fighting to drag himself to safety before those murderous hobnails could trample him down. Near him, powder was hissing — in his nostrils the smell of scorched fuse jacket. For some reason he noticed those things.

He felt the impact of Brunner's boot. It drove his head to one side. His fingers almost slipped from the log's wet, cold surface. He grabbed again, barely saving himself. Brunner leaped in, smashing the boot again and again, and each time Tim's fingers loosened a trifle more.

He fell, came to a stop, was imprisoned, wedged deeply. The roar of water was all around him. Flowing over him. Tangled logs prevented the current sweeping him away. Instinct made him climb. There was an obstruction above. A length of white pine log almost two feet in diameter. He tried to lift it, but it didn't budge.

He set his feet, took a deep breath, and heaved with a mighty straightening of his legs and back. The log rolled. It seemed like a minute that he'd been imprisoned, but actually it had been no more than six seconds. Brunner, seeing him disappear, had immediately turned his attention to the fuse.

It had burned from sight, leaving a black shell of casing to mark its position. He stepped on the log, and Tim, rising, made it spin underfoot. He saw Tim clawing his way into sight. He tried to get up, to swing those boots again. His foot was wedged. It took him a couple seconds to rip it free. The young man was already standing, waiting for him.

Brunner was up with a lunge, but this time the advantages of balance and footing were on the other side. A left met his advance, rocking him to one side, and then a right struck, stunning and abrupt, like the blow of an axe. Brunner flung up his arms in a desperate effort to save himself. It would have been better for him had he fallen. Chipman, realizing his advantage, found new footing, shifted his weight. His feet were wide, his hobnails set. He swung again with all the whiplash strength of his body. The blow landed flush on the jaw. It knocked Brunner flat. He lay on his back, arms flung wide.

Tim Chipman could have gone in and finished him with his hobnails. Instead, he waited while Brunner rolled over, crawled to a kneeling position, and thence to his feet. Brunner's wandering eyes came to rest on Tim, and with a slow movement he tried to lift his guard. Tim brushed it aside and smashed a right and left that rocked his head as though his neck had turned to rubber.

Brunner crawled. His mashed lips formed words: "No. You're being . . . fool. Pull the fuse. Both of us . . . get killed."

He started toward the fuse, fell face down, his hands deeply among the logs, among close-set cases of powder. Chipman seized him by the collar, dragged him up, balanced him on wobbly legs, and struck him down.

Brunner made it on hands and knees to the crest of the log jam. His lips kept forming the words: "No, no!" In his eyes now an awful, animal fear.

He staggered to his feet. He was at the crest of the jam. And at that instant explosion struck.

The force of concussion knocked Tim forward. He was down and picking himself up. Beneath him, through the tangled cribwork of logs, he could still hear the hissing fuse. The explosion had come from that charge Jorgensen had set off. This main blast could be no more than a few seconds away. He saw Brunner trip and fall. He thought the man was coming back to make another attempt at the fuse. Even now, Tim Chipman had no thought of pulling it. Breaking the jam had become the sole purpose of his life. But Brunner was not coming that way. He tried to run along the crests. In his mind now only the desperate thought of escape.

A log turned underfoot, set him face foremost to the river. Both log and man disappeared. The log bobbed in sight, with Brunner clinging to it. Tim started for the cañon wall, taking long strides. He clambered up — ten, twenty feet. There was a ledge, a crevice where tangled juniper had taken root. The explosion hit. It hurled him face down. He was gently sliding through loose rocks and juniper. He came to a stop, turned, holding to a branch with one hand.

The air was filled with roaring wood fragments. All around him the sudden, pitchy smell of new pine. The log jam seemed unchanged for a moment, then it bellied out and was gone downriver with a massive roll. Tim clambered upward from the little gully, found support, and got to one knee. The river was a mass of bobbing logs.

A movement caught his eye. Brunner ahead of the logs, wading waist deep toward shore. A log bore down on him. It batted him under, but he came up again. He was clawing for the rocks. There was no handhold. He kept slipping. Then Tim saw someone else. A huge man, running along the shore. Axe-Handle Ole.

Ole got footing, reached far out. Brunner seized the hand, staggered to his feet, waded the waist-deep current. When he was close enough, Axe-Handle suddenly bent, seized Brunner by his shirt and the crotch of his pants. For a second, Brunner was high over his head. Then, with a bellow that could be heard above the thunder of wood and water, Ole hurled him far out into the bobbing crush of logs.

Tim stood for a long time, waiting for Brunner to reappear. He never would. No man can fall through the close-locked press of such a drive and live.

At noon the last log had disappeared downcañon, and by night the first of them would be bobbing to rest against the ice that still clutched the shores of Beaver Lake. It would be another month before they could be herded together in rafts to be towed by a steam tug down to the Macardle mills. But the battle was won, and Brunner, had he been alive, could never have stopped them.

In a way, Tim was sorry the man couldn't be around. He'd wanted to smash his business and drive him from the country. He was thinking about that as he stood with Lynne Tilton near the cañon crest, watching the afternoon sun pick up bits of ice shine from the swift-flowing river below.

"We could have broken him, you and I," he said. "We could do anything together."

"Don't talk about him," she said coldly. "Don't talk about anything but us. The two of us."

About the Author

Dan Cushman was born in Osceola, Michigan, and grew up on the Cree Indian Reservation in Montana. He graduated from the University of Montana with a Bachelor of Science degree in 1934 and pursued a career in mining as a prospector, assayer, and geologist before turning to journalism. In the early 1940s his novelette-length stories began appearing regularly in such Fiction House magazines as *North-West Romances* and *Frontier Stories*. Later in the decade his North-Western and Western stories as well as fiction set in the Far East and Africa began appearing in *Action Stories*, *Adventure*, and *Short Stories*. *Stay Away, Joe*, which first appeared in 1953, is an amusing novel about the mixture, and occasional collision, of Indian culture and Anglo-American culture among the Métis (French Indians) living on a reservation in Montana. The novel became a bestseller and remains a classic to this day, greatly loved especially by Indian peoples for its truthfulness and humor. Yet, while humor became Cushman's hallmark in such later novels as *The Old Copper Collar* (1957) and *Good Bye, Old Dry* (1959), he also produced significant historical fiction in *The Silver Mountain* (1957), concerned with the mining and politics of silver in Montana in the 1890s. This novel won a Spur Award from the Western Writers of America. His fiction remains notable for its breadth, ranging all the way from a story of the cattle frontier in *Tall Wyoming* (1957) to a poignant and memorable portrait of small-town life in Michigan just before the Great War in *The Grand and the Glorious* (1963). He also wrote *White Water Trail*.